# Phoenix
# No
# More

# Phoenix No More

## by
## EDWIN GAGE

HARPER & ROW, PUBLISHERS
New York, Hagerstown,
San Francisco, London

# A HARPER NOVEL OF SUSPENSE

Grateful acknowledgment is made for permission to reprint the following:

Excerpt from *The Odyssey*, translated by Robert Fitzgerald. Copyright © 1961 by Robert Fitzgerald. Reprinted by permission of Doubleday & Company, Inc.

Excerpt from *To Have or to Be?* by Erich Fromm, Volume Fifty, from the World Perspective Series, edited by Ruth Nanda Anshen. Copyright © 1976 by Erich Fromm. Reprinted by permission of Harper & Row, Publishers, Inc.

FIRST EDITION

*Designed by Eve Kirch Callahan*

Library of Congress Cataloging in Publication Data

Gage, Edwin.
  Phoenix no more.
  I. Title.
PZ4.G1295.Ph 1978    [PS3557.A326]    813'.5'4
ISBN 0-06-011403-7    77-11787

78 79 80 81 82 10 9 8 7 6 5 4 3 2 1

*To Doris and Ken, and to all living crea-*
*tures still unborn who deserve a better*
*world then we will leave them.*

# Part One

He saw the townlands
and learned the minds of many distant men,
and weathered many bitter nights and days
in his deep heart at sea, while he fought only
to save his life, to bring his shipmates home.
But not by will nor valor could he save them,
for their own recklessness destroyed them all—
children and fools, they filled and feasted on
the cattle of Lord Helios, the Sun,
and he who moves all day through heaven
took from their eyes the dawn of their return.

> Homer,
> *The Odyssey*

*"Nuclear waste is the most eternal product of man's genius. Long after the pyramids are reduced to sand, which has been carried a grain at a time by a tiny bird across the ocean to make a new desert, nuclear waste will still be destroying its own containers and leaking out to destroy life."*

> Cass Boulding, speaking in his
> private diary, March 29, 1977

"What is past is past, and the damage we may already have done to future generations cannot be rescinded, but we cannot shirk the compelling responsibility to determine if the course we are following is one we should be following."

> Thruston B. Morton of Kentucky,
> speaking to Congress, February 29, 1968

*"In short, nothing serious is being done to plan for the survival of the human race."*

> Erich Fromm,
> *To Have or to Be*

# 1

The wind was down and the dust had fallen. I was lying naked on a hot boulder, and I felt the sun's rays untie deep knots in my muscles. Turning my closed eyes in the direction of the light, I watched my eyelids become furnace red. My eye sockets relaxed and I saw fragments of my recent life flicker on a red screen.

I was tired and city damaged and I needed a rest.

I dreamed a while before I came awake, shook off my sleep and looked down from the boulder. In the far distance Phoenix was spread out beneath me like a large topographical map. A silver-flashing military jet sprang from a distant airport as though shot from a bow. It was a rare clear day, and the first in many weeks without cold winds howling. Buzzards rode the shimmering air currents all around.

I lay back down, drowsy again, until my dog growled. He was a few feet away from me on the edge of the boulder looking toward Phoenix. The tone of his growl was intimate, meant only for me to hear: a warning.

"Good boy, Bandit, now quiet." I reached across the rock for my pants and took my gun and crawled over next to him. Stroking the back of his spotted neck, I looked to see what he was watching.

About a quarter-mile away, a young woman, hiking alone through the desert, was approaching us. She walked with her eyes to the ground, and when I took up my binoculars I could see she was following my barefoot prints across the rock and sand. She stopped, shaded her eyes and scanned the hillside.

I squatted so she could not see me.

"Temperamental bastard," she muttered. Sound carries well in the desert.

Her footsteps were crashing up over the small rocks when, still out of her sight, I slipped into my pants.

Halfway up the hill, still tracking me, she called in exasperation, "Mr. Falconer! Mr. Falconer!"

I rose and looked at her through my binoculars. Perspiration was running down her cheeks, down the creases of her nose to bead on her upper lip. Her lips were fleshy and strong, her eyes fierce and beautiful.

"Where did you learn to track?" I asked.

She'd seen me.

"Horses," she said. "When I was a kid we had spooky horses that didn't like to be ridden. I need to talk to you. Now are you gonna come down or do I have to come up?"

I didn't answer and she spent another ten minutes scrambling, cursing and stumbling through the loose rocks on the side of the hill before she reached me. She

4

seemed to be a strong woman and it was a pleasure to watch her battle gravity and dodge cactus.

I had seen one other woman in my life who'd attracted me immediately as much as Jinks Boulding had. The other woman had had fine Indian almond skin and features, and she had smiled at me from a street corner in downtown Phoenix as I'd waited at a red light. By the time I had driven my truck over a curb and into a flower bed to park it, she had disappeared. I'd loitered around the corner for days hoping she would pass by again.

"How'd you know where to look for me?" I asked.

"Your truck was in the driveway, so I walked around your house. I found your barefoot prints leading off into the desert and figured you couldn't go far. Good reasoning; wrong results. You've got tough feet. Have you decided to go totally wild? I was worried I might find you naked."

"You almost did. Look, I told your mother I'm taking the year off."

"She thought I might be able to convince you to postpone your vacation a while longer. She knows you by reputation, and she wants you to protect my father."

"I don't like your father."

"How could you not like him? You don't know him."

"In some ways I know him better than you do. I investigated him while I was working for the prosecutor's office. He stole more money that year than I'll make in my lifetime."

Startled into silence by my bluntness, she bit her lip, deciding something. She had not introduced herself because that wasn't necessary. I had seen her lovely face

5

smiling at me several hundred times. On the front of her album covers her face was always thoughtful, serene and slightly breathless. The frequent feature articles in the Sunday section of the Phoenix Sun heaped the predictable praise on the hometown girl made good as a Hollywood singer.

Jinks Boulding was better known than our state senators or supreme court justices. She came from an old Phoenix family who had owned a large ranch west of the city. About two hundred thousand acres of that land had been converted into suburbia by the family construction company.

"Ordinarily," she said, "I wouldn't do something like this. But when you told Mother you didn't want to work for a year, she asked me to try to persuade you. Ordinarily she's too proud to ask me to do something because she can't do it, but she's convinced that someone is going to kill Dad."

Beyond the curve her neck made with her shoulder, another jet sprang into the air, and around us a wind blew lightly. I saw the worry in Jinks's face, and knew that if I went on with this conversation I would be working again soon.

"She thinks someone wants to kill her husband, Cass Boulding?" I asked with that inane repetition of one caught only half listening, not wanting to listen at all.

"Ex."

"Her ex-husband, your father?"

"Yes."

"Have there been threats?"

"I guess you could say the threats came to her in a

dream. They didn't come by something as mundane as a phone call or a note. But I'm afraid I believe in her dreams."

"Is it possible that *she's* mad at her ex-husband and wants to murder him?" I asked.

I expected my question to unleash an angry flood and end this temptation to work before it started. Then I could go back to soaking up the sun.

"That is quite possible," she said. "When she asked me to come speak to you, I asked her the same sort of question. She said no. I told her I'd need more than her word because I didn't want to make a fool of myself in front of you, and so she allowed me to talk to her psychiatrist about it. In private."

Beyond the base of our hill, on the flat desert plane, paloverde trees bent double as a sudden March wind approached from nowhere, dragging its curtain of dust.

"And the doctor said these dreams are telling her the truth?"

Jinks spoke slowly, I thought, not from any hestitation or lack of belief in what she was saying, but so that I would have time to understand. "He didn't discount it, nor did he claim it was true. He said she has these premonitions, of that there's no real doubt because she reports them. And he said she's been accurate in the past. Whether they are coming from her imagination or from some other source he's not willing to say."

"I don't believe in that stuff," I said. "She doesn't need me; she needs a better shrink."

"I don't believe in it either, because it's never happened to me, but the doctor said he won't pretend to know what he doesn't know, which is what you are doing."

I stood up, stung by a jolt that went through my muscles. I felt a vague fear as the little wind that had been crossing the plain had reached us full of stinging dust. I felt Jinks was thinking more clearly than I was and I was impatient at myself and admiring her.

"What am I doing?"

"You claim to know what she is experiencing, yet you haven't talked to her. The doctor doesn't know the answer, nor does he claim he knows it. In that sense he is smarter than you, because by admitting his ignorance, he's ready to learn."

Even though the sun was still hot, the air had chilled me and I stood listening to this woman and I wanted to go on listening.

# 2

Jinks Boulding drove over the gravel road with the same speed and abandon as she'd drive a paved road. Out of the back window I watched the curtain of dust that was leaping up behind us. For a long while we had been tearing across the Boulding ranch road at speeds which set my toes clenching. As we rounded a sharp left curve and dropped into an arroyo and leaped up the opposite bank, Jinks stole a glance at me and said, "Don't worry. I've been driving this road since I was ten. I can do it with my eyes closed."

"Think I'll try that," I said. Her laughter warmed me and I added, "I like your songs."

"Which ones?"

"Your good ones. 'Open Windows,' 'Hostages to Fate,' 'Innocent Bystanders.'"

"Those are my best. But I couldn't have sold an album without the others, the clichés."

"Well, I like your good ones," I said.

The road leveled out on a flat plane and in the distance I could see a large brick arch spanning the road. On top of the arch I could already make out the letters, ORO ESTE.

A pack of ranch dogs attacked the truck as Jinks climbed out. They yapped and yawned and shivered with excitement to see her, and she told a mean-looking Doberman that I was a friend and that he must not gnaw on my throat.

Instead of walking toward the house, she moved off toward a barn and a set of corrals to the left and I followed, admiring her fluid and decisive legs.

She climbed up and sat on the top rail of the corral fence and a look of affection transformed her face as she watched a Mexican cowboy working a sorrel quarter-horse filly that had only recently been tamed. The filly's eyes flashed and the muscles beneath her glistening skin shivered because there was still a tension between her will and the will of the man on her back. He reined her one way and then the other, gentle but firm, talking softly to her.

After a while, he rode over to where we were watching and pulled, up saying, "*Qué tal, Jinks?* Sure is a pretty girl, no?"

"Pretty as her momma," said Jinks. Then to me, "Her momma was Clytemnestra, her daddy Julius Caesar."

"Quite an ancestry."

"Chato, this is Mr. Falconer. He's a friend of mine."

"Of course," said Chato, to the back of the filly's head. He was one of those shy, gentle men who understands horses, and so when talking to a strange man must look at a horse.

"I want you to know," she said to me, "that Chato is the only man I would let touch Pandora. I broke her myself, with some guidance from Chato, of course. No one knows horses like he does."

Chato examined one of his stirrups to hide his embarrassment. His brown hairless hands rested on top of the saddle horn, and his brown eyes were quiet as the eyes of his naked ancestors as they watched the first ridiculous black-frocked Catholic fathers toiling through the desert on a mission to save heathen souls.

"About the accuracy of Mother's dreams," said Jinks as we walked toward the ranch house. "I'm probably not a good judge. When I was a child I saw her predict some things which I still can't explain."

"Like what?"

"Years ago she and Dad were sleeping side by side one night when she dreamed his fist was coming down toward her. Her hands jerked up to protect herself, and she woke up catching his hand just inches above her face. He woke up, too, and told her he was dreaming that he was about to hit her but couldn't stop himself. He hoped she would awaken and stop him."

Jinks spoke as we walked and I listened without comment. I felt a certain awe of her mother's clairvoyance, but that wasn't the most interesting part of the incident for me.

"Who told you this?"

"Both of them. And there were other instances."

The Doberman had been following us at a distance, eyeing me as if his teeth itched. I glared at him to let him know I could not be intimidated. We crossed a broad, open expanse of tan foot-worn earth between the barn and the house, and buzzards rode the currents above, rising and falling in the sudden gusts. Jinks stopped and pointed to the side of a hill about a quarter of a mile away to where two coyotes stood looking sideways down at us. All around were small bursts of dust as though invisible footsteps were driven by the wind.

We entered a cavernous living room. The walls were made of metamorphic rock collected from the mountains. They were red, purple and mustard colored. Above was a heavy-beamed ceiling, below was a shining hardwood floor, with Navajo rugs placed around it.

Two Mexican women were busily stringing crepe paper streamers and tacking them to the ceiling beams. Another woman was standing on a chair driving a nail into one of the beams. She was having trouble with the hammer, so Jinks went and helped her. Together they hung a large donkey *piñata* from the middle of the room.

"Dad's birthday tomorrow," said Jinks.

"What's your mother doing giving a party for her ex-husband?"

"Just because they're no longer married doesn't mean she no longer loves him."

At the other end of the room Sheila Boulding lounged on a mountain-lion skin. In front of her was a roaring mesquite fire. Something very intense and interesting must have been happening between those flaming logs and among the small flaring red and yellow flames because she didn't seem to notice us until, we had been seated for some time behind her.

We sat there in silence until she turned, rose and I was introduced.

This woman who owned more land than a small European country was dressed in cowboy boots, worn Levi's, a snap-buttoned shirt and a mink stole. Her voice was scratchy, dried by the desert winds, and her eyes, like her daughter's, were darting and intense when she looked at me.

"So, Mr. Falconer, you have decided to work this year after all," she said.

"Jinks tracked me down. I didn't have a chance."

She smiled, "Would you like a drink?"

"No thank you. I was wondering if you could tell me why you think someone would want to harm Cass Boulding?"

"Then you are planning to protect him."

"First I need to know something about what I'm protecting him from."

"For the past few days, I've had a strong feeling, very strong, that I have had only a few times in my life. It comes to me only before the death of someone I love. The first time it came was shortly before my father died. The next time I had the feeling was shortly before my Uncle Fred's death."

Her gaze drifted back to the fire, and I could tell I was in for a long list of her dream experiences, all of which would be useless to me because there was no way to verify them. I was more interested in what I thought she was holding back than in what she was telling me now.

"Jinks told me about the time you dreamed your husband was about to hit you and you awoke in time to catch his fist."

"And that one, too," she said.

"Why do you think he was so mad?" I asked.

Her eyes flashed and her lower jaw shifted into an angry position before she caught herself. She said, "That was a long time ago. It was just some little thing, something all married couples go through."

I said nothing. She looked at me, then said with exaggerated concern, "Your face, Mr. Falconer, looks a bit burnt. Don't tell me you've been careless with the sun."

# 3

An armed guard emerged from the guardhouse and Jinks slowed the car to give him a smile. He brightened and waved us by and I bounced between the seat and the ceiling as she drove too fast over the gravel road. A line of workmen's trucks streamed past us going in the opposite direction. Many of the men in bouncing trucks recognized Jinks and waved and whooped and hollered. The dust was so thick my teeth screeched against each other. It was impossible not to grind them at such speeds.

"If anyone is there with him, we'll make like you're my boyfriend," she told me, swooping to a stop alongside an enormous construction trailer.

"Nobody'll believe it. I'm too ugly."

"Loving ugly men builds character," she said. "Anyone can love a beautiful man."

"You were supposed to correct me."

"I never correct anyone," she said and smiled at me.

The Boulding Brothers Construction trailer was one of

the many temporary office buildings the various construction contractors had clustered to the east of the Phoenix Nuclear Facility. Following Jinks, I glanced up at the metal gridwork of the half-constructed plant and was startled. It was larger than I had ever imagined anything except a mountain could be. The bulldozers creeping over the landscape at its base seemed like toys and the workers were not recognizable as men; they were more like insects.

My attention was still on the power plant when Jinks stopped and I, following her without watching, bumped into her back. I apologized. We were on the front steps of the Boulding Brothers Construction trailer. Dust rose in small bursts all across the disturbed earth of the construction site.

"What do you mean, I should talk him out of hating you?" The voice was penetrating the flimsy walls of the trailer. "Of course he respects me; *I've* treated *him* with respect."

The voice paused. Its tone was ironic and mocking, a controlled rage. I bumped into Jinks again, mumbled an excuse, then realized *I* was standing still and she was *backing* away from the trailer, pushing me back down the steps.

The voice had begun to roar as we moved toward Jinks's car: "Goddammit, I already did you a big favor when I didn't blow your brains out. Now I've made my peace with the powers that be and with him, and you're just going to have to live with yourself. That's all! I've got too much on my mind to be fooling around with *your* nonsense."

The voice reached a roar of rage, then silence from the trailer.

"What's *that* all about?" I asked.

"Don't know," she said, without turning toward me, and then she once again climbed the steps. As she opened the door she said loudly, "Hi, Dad."

I followed slowly, as I felt Jinks wanted to talk to her father alone, and I wandered through a door to my left into the blueprint room. In it were half a dozen large high tables with all sorts of attachments for examining blueprints, and I found a four-by-eight-foot artist's model of the power plant. Looking closer, I saw a red X marking the *you-are-here* spot, where I was inside a trailer looking at the artist's model of the nuclear power plant.

I heard Jinks and Cass Boulding exchange greetings and then there was silence in the other room except for a number of military jets which flew overhead. Their vicious sound set coyotes howling in the desert. They were moving in for the night hunting of the rodents made homeless by the day's bulldozing.

Jinks came to find me in the blueprint room.

"What's up?" I asked.

"He's thinking about something."

"Doesn't he stop thinking when his famous daughter comes for a visit?"

"No. When he plunges into thought, he is visiting someplace else. He's been like this, dropping into deep thought, almost trances, for several years. It's the way I am when a new song comes to me."

"Does he write songs while he's ignoring his daughter?"

Ignoring my sarcasm, she explained, "No. Because he doesn't know music; that's not his medium. But he's doing the same thing, really, in his own way, with his own tools."

"Jinks, what are you doing in there?" boomed Cass Boulding's voice. Gone now was the rage I heard earlier, when he was talking on the phone.

She introduced me.

Cass Boulding looked at me and his eyes did a little jump. I guessed he was remembering my investigation of him when I worked for the prosecutor's office. We had never been introduced, but he had seen me fairly often, and at the time, I found out later, the Boulding Brothers had spies of their own, so I imagined he knew all about my reports on his activities.

As crooks went, Cass Boulding was one of the more honest. As far as I could tell he never paid for a murder. Most of the money he stole came from what was known as "Short Work" in the prosecutor's office, which involves collusion between engineers and contractors. The engineers design work with twice the necessary strength, and the contractors build at less than required strength. The gap in wages and materials between what is called for in the plans and the actual construction cost runs into millions of dollars cash per month for an outfit the size of Boulding Brothers. Once this untaxable cash is distributed, tongues and cement harden at the same rate.

The contemplative look still in his eyes, Cass asked me, "Did you know that an American anthropologist recently gave a metal ax to a man in a stone ax tribe in Australia? The man with the metal ax soon proved it could break

18

stone axes by breaking the chief's ax and then killing him, and then followed strife, disease, and the eventual disintegration of the tribe and death of everyone in it."

"No, I didn't know that," I said.

"Did you know that the San Francisco dock workers used to unload ships with muscle power, but then the companies automated the process, electrified it, and the dock workers developed much higher rates of heart disease? So the deal is: we pay for electricity with heart disease?"

"I didn't know that either."

"Then you're not smart enough for my daughter. Get rid of him, Jinks."

"Dad, this is Daniel Falconer. He's not my boyfriend."

She told him about Sheila Boulding's dreams, and about her hiring me.

"Damned witch," he muttered. There was more affection for his ex-wife in his voice than I had expected, but there was no affection when he said to me, "You're fired." The sun was setting. He reached over and turned on a light so that I could see the determination in his face and know he meant what he said.

"You didn't hire me," I said. "If you don't want protection, you can speak to Mrs. Boulding about it and she'll tell me."

"You dog my footsteps and I'll have you bruised."

Turning to Jinks, he poked himself in the middle of his chest with his index finger and said, "I've got the answers here. Now, honey, please don't get in my way while I do what must be done."

"Dad, we're only trying to help—"

"You try to help me now and you'll only interfere." Several times he poked his chest with his index finger for emphasis as he spoke.

"Won't you listen—"

"Get outta my way, woman. You're jumping off the diving board without checking to see if the pool has any water." He was bent forward then, speaking passionately with his eyes and hands until my presence once again seeped into his awareness. He tossed an ugly glance in my direction and quit poking himself in the chest.

"I mean it. I don't even want to see you again," he said to me.

Soon after I arrived home that night I received a call from Sheila. Jinks had told her the results of our meeting with Cass, and Sheila wanted to make sure I would continue working for her. I told her that in view of my past dealings with her husband and his feelings toward me I didn't think I was the best man to do the work she wanted done. She offered more money. By that time I had emptied three beer cans and the whole thing sounded pretty crazy, but I said I would keep working anyway. I told her that I would begin the next day, trying to find out what Cass Boulding was doing that might endanger him.

# 4

I had parked my truck on the county road about three miles' crow-flight from Cass Boulding's new house, the one he had recently built on another of his ranches when his divorce proceedings began. I was carrying binoculars because I wanted to see how he lived and what he did. Jinks had shown me on a topographical map the exact location of his house, and she had described his security precautions, which included electronic sensing devices along the road, the brother of the Doberman who had eyed me at her mother's house, and his No Visitors policy.

Jinks told me the No Visitors policy was nearly total. Not even she was allowed to visit his new house. Only Chato, who had worked for Cass Boulding for more than thirty years, was free to come and go. Chato divided his attention between the work he did at both houses.

I hiked to the top of the hill above the ranch house and sat down in the shade of a cactus and took out my binoculars. I would not be able to approach any closer, which was just a little over a quarter mile, because the desert was barren and I would be seen if I came over the top of the hill.

The sun was white at noon. There were no shadows nor promise of shadows in the eye-squinting brightness. Small desert bushes tossed like waves in the gusts of wind.

Cass Boulding's new ranch house and barns were nearly a duplicate of the ones he'd left behind. The positioning of the barns and corrals and house was the same, but there was something stark, almost naked about the new house. Then I realized that the peach trees in the backyard and the cottonwood trees in the front were fifty years younger than the trees at the other ranch.

I had been watching for a half hour when a pickup truck drove up the road and parked in front of the house. Chato got out and walked to the barn where three horses stood in a metal corral. Several dogs, one of them a Doberman, ran from the front yard and escorted Chato across the open space where he passed through a gate and approached the horses.

He was carrying grain to them in a metal bucket when Cass Boulding emerged from the house. After Chato finished graining the horses, the two men stood and talked across the corral fence. The Doberman ran back and forth across the clearing, with his nose in the air, and I worried he might have been picking up my scent. Then I realized there was no danger because the wind was switching directions every minute or so and to the black dog's nose, if he'd caught my scent, I must have been coming from everywhere and going everywhere at once.

The green metal barn was large for a ranch with only three horses, but I knew Cass Boulding did things in a big way. When investigating him I found out that he had grown up on a ranch larger than Rhode Island, and he and his friends had, in the space of twenty years, built Phoenix into a city of one million. If he wanted a barn the size of a gymnasium, he would have one, as another man might have a sports car, I thought, and felt the chill on the back of my neck.

Chato was sliding the door along the overhead metal tracks. It stuck on something and Cass had to lend a shoulder to shove it open. Then they both disappeared into the barn.

A few minutes later Chato emerged carrying two large briefcases. He was slightly stooped from their weight. Cass followed with a smaller briefcase under one arm. With his free hand he shoved the sliding door closed and locked it, and followed Chato across the open space to the house.

The wind was freezing the back of my neck and I was thinking that maybe two large briefcases and one small one contained more than just hay bills.

I turned up my coat collar to protect my neck. My eyes were burning from so much intense concentration and I had to rest them. I raised them from the tunnels of the binoculars, and I saw the black Doberman coming in my direction like an arrow. The wind blew against the back of my head and I realized suddenly that it had shifted, and had tricked me. Briefly I prayed to it to switch directions, but it blew steadily on.

The dog grew larger, galloping across an arroyo and up my hill. I looked around for something to climb, but there was nothing but cactus. The Doberman was running toward me, making no sounds. I kept waiting for him to stop and bark and defend territory, but he came steadily on the attack.

I rose and began running down the side of the hill, hoping a scrub or mesquite would shoot instantly out of the earth. I realized that if I didn't think clearly the dog would kill me. I ripped off my jacket and rolled it around my forearm as the dog came over the top of the hill and stopped for a moment, looking down at me. We were about fifty feet apart, staring at each other, and he still hadn't made a sound.

He was on a downhill run now while I raised my covered arm as a shield and whirled the binoculars around my head on their cord. He approached in a series of jerking still photographs as I slowed time and swung the binoculars in giant arcs and synchronized my last three swings with his last ten steps, as if trying to bat a baseball out of the air before it hit my face. I missed. Instead of cracking against the side of his head to the left of his eyes, they caught him in the neck. Something hit me in the chest and I was flying backward, amazed and gasping, amazed there was no air in my lungs while teeth were snapping in front of my face. I hit the desert flat on my back, knocking air out of my chest as he disappeared over my left shoulder. I rose up gasping and trying to turn to meet him, but the air would not enter my chest fast enough. He landed and whirled and lunged toward my face. I was on my hands and knees still trying to take the first breath of air since he hit me and there was nothing I cared more about than this taking in of air, though my arm was raised to fill his mouth. He heaved my arm from side to side. His teeth hit the bone of my forearm and I could feel my shoulder in its socket. It was an old instinct, this shaking of a prey to break its neck, one learned before his immediate ancestors were bred by Nazis for killing men. My shoulder slapped in its socket and my elbow was bending oddly. Suddenly, my breathlessness diminished and my lungs expanded. I rose up on my knees, gave the binoculars one free turn for momentum and brought them down in the middle of his skull. He fell and yelped, shaking his head as I gave the binoculars another wild swing and brought them down on top of his head again.

# 5

I hate doctors. The worse I hurt the more I hate doctors. All I wanted was a lockjaw shot, but the sadist I went to wanted to move my shoulder around to see if it was dislocated. I told him it wasn't broken and when he was fooling with it I told him I would break his elbow if he didn't leave mine alone. He told jokes and laughed at me while he was sewing up some of the larger holes in my arm. He suggested rabies shots, but I told him I'd fallen on rusty nails, a whole board full of them. After that he was silent for a while, before he said I was the only patient he ever had who lied about a dog attack. Finally it seemed to dawn on him that I wanted him to shut up.

I went home and drank pain-killer-on-ice and watched all the vile, vicious, vapid filth I could find on television. I had a craving for pollution inversions and oil spills. I'd watch a minute of that and then switch to a quiz program full of mindless fools screaming about meaningless prizes. Then to a comedy where canned laughter synchronized with the throbbing in my arm.

When my rage at being attacked began to pass, Bandit came over and licked my ear. I sat up on the couch and stroked the back of his neck and had to chuckle at the look of pleasure on his masked face. Just looking at him always made me smile.

If Bandit had been given to me I would have named him Clown because his face looked like the clown dancers in Hopi festivals. But since I had stolen him, I named him Bandit, which also suited his looks.

He was purebred Dalmation, but all the spots on his face had gathered together around his eyes to form a mask. I had met him one night when I went to visit an ex-friend who had purebred dalmations. Then the largest pup in a litter of six, he had tottered over to me and licked my hand and my ex-friend had said he was going to drown that one because of his flawed face. I told my ex-friend to give me the pup to save himself the ordeal of drowning him, that, having a flawed face myself, I didn't begrudge it in others. Nothing doing, he said. He didn't want the pup's genes running around ready to pollute the pure genes of his other dogs. I persisted, reminding my ex-friend that his own face was not without flaws. My ex-friend relented, saying he would compromise. He would castrate the dog, and then both of us could be happy. I said I didn't think the pup would be happy. I went out to my truck and got a bottle of bourbon and fed drinks to my ex-friend until he passed out. Then I stole Bandit. The next morning my ex-friend must have known what had happened, but who wants to accuse an ex-friend of stealing a puppy already promised as a gift?

I put Bandit outside and lay back down on the couch and nodded off for a while. I awoke from Bandit's barking and hoped it was Cass Boulding in the approaching car and that Bandit would find his ankle bone. But it wasn't Cass. It was Jinks. When she got out of her car Bandit quit barking and sniffed her thighs.

She was surprised by my bandages and questioned me, but I brushed her off with the rusty nail story. In the desert, coyotes and buzzards were now eating the carcass of that son-of-a-bitch, and I didn't want anyone giving him a decent burial.

She sat beside me on the couch and searched my eyes for a while before she decided to accept my lie about the nails, then told me what she had come to tell me, that Sheila wanted me to attend Cass's birthday party that evening as Jinks's boyfriend and to be Cass's inconspicuous bodyguard.

I reminded her that Cass Boulding didn't want to see me anymore, and she told me her father would be civil to me as long as I was at her mother's house. Besides, she said, she had told her father that she really was dating me. She hoped I didn't mind.

I asked her what the hell was her mother doing giving birthday parties for an ex-husband.

"One of the mysteries of unhealed love," she said and put her head on my shoulder. "You thought all those sad love songs I did came out of my love life, didn't you? Didn't you?"

# 6

Rounding the last curve before the arch, I saw Jinks walking between parked cars to meet me. She stopped next to the governor's limousine, watching me while I looked for a place to park.

There were cars all over the Boulding homestead. Cars in the gardens, cars in the corrals, cars in the barns and cars lining the road. This was not going to be any simple family shindig. For Cass Boulding, even a birthday party became an affair of state.

I parked in back of a long line, pulling my truck off the side of the road into the desert.

I liked that space; in case of stampede, I would not get tangled in traffic. Long ago I learned to sit near exits and park in the back.

Jinks took my arm and we were passing between cars when Chato came around a corner of the house and headed toward the corrals. He was wearing his work clothes and a sweat-rimmed old Stetson, and he was so deep in thought he didn't see us. Jinks hailed him and he stopped and stared at the ground.

"Chato! Aren't you coming to the party?"

"I better doctor your filly a little bit before it gets too dark. I barely had any time to check on her at all these last couple days."

"She told me she's okay and she wants you to come to Dad's party."

He didn't even smile. Apparently the filly talked to him, too. "I barely had time to rub her today." He was still staring at the ground, firm in his resolve.

Jinks and I walked into the front yard, holding hands for effect.

"You treat the help like that and they'll get uppity," I said.

"It hasn't ruined you yet."

I smiled at her. She told me earlier that Chato had taught her to ride and understand horses and that as a small child she had thought of him as a man superior to either her father or Uncle Claude. In fact, she said, in her childhood feelings, she had taken his humility and gentleness with her and animals as a sign of true value, and for a while she had loved him more than her father or uncle because they were always so distant, so preoccupied with getting more property. But as she grew up, Chato had begun to react to her as though she too were one of his employers. That made her sad.

As we approached the house, leafless branches above were swinging wildly in the wind. Darkness was coming in nearly visible steps on the desert, and in the distance coyotes were howling.

Once inside the house, Jinks pulled me on a beeline toward her brother, Joshua.

Even before we were introduced, I found him interesting. Unlike the other guests at the party who were all dressed in whatever expensive clothing they considered fashionable, Joshua wore heavy boots as worn as Van Gogh's, patched Levi's and a green plaid shirt with the sleeves rolled up to the elbows of his strong, round, hairy arms. As Jinks was introducing him, I smelled his heavy man-odor of accumulated perspiration. It was strong, and it was out of place since everyone else was properly powdered and perfumed.

Our glances surprised one another when I looked above his bush of black beard and caught an unmistakable line—a family resemblance—to Sheila and Jinks around his eye sockets. And in the eyes themselves, which seemed to have a life of their own independent of the rest of his face, there was a concentrated fierceness, almost a madness, accentuated by his dark-arched eyebrows.

After introducing us, Jinks went off in search of her father, and Joshua said to me, "You look as if you feel like a bastard son at a family reunion."

"These aren't exactly my people."

"Be proud to have the right enemies. The wrong friends is the second worst curse on earth. Second only to the wrong family. Your name sounds familiar. Who are you?"

"Jinks told you. Her boyfriend."

"You'll recover."

Joshua Boulding invited people to like or despise him

immediately. I liked him, but I could imagine that a lot of people didn't.

"Do you realize," he asked, "that the desert wasn't made for civilization?" He watched me carefully to see my reaction. "This instant city we are building is transforming the most beautiful place on earth into the ugliest. In green zones there is something to balance the harsh, angular materials man uses to construct his shit beetle city. But in the desert the finest qualities are the vast emptiness and the mystical solitude, which are destroyed automatically by industrial civilization. The scary part is that modern man is becoming so dependent on his gadgets, and all animals on earth are becoming dependent on man."

As he spoke, his dark eyes slammed shut and open in a spasmodic tic he had in which his forehead shot down to meet his uprising cheeks. There was an intensity about him that seemed to sweat sparks, like a red horseshoe fresh from a blacksmith's forge.

"Ha," he said, "Yesterday I spent the day up in the mountains watching shit beetles feed their city. Homer and me sat down on a flat rock next to a cow plop and watched it quiver. You ever see a cow plop quiver? Well, it quivers for a while, then in one place a piece of it breaks loose, about the size of a marble, and rolls away from the mass. Following this marble is a shit beetle—scarabs if you're a bible nut—who's standing on his hind legs. He has his front legs up on top of his prize, and he packs it the way a kid packs the top of the snowball he's going to use for the body of a snowman. That's the way Mr. Scarab does, rolling along his ball of shit that's tall as his eyeballs, pack, pack, so it doesn't break apart. He looks like an orchestra conductor with his tails, pushing along this giant brown snowball until it hits a rock and rolls back over the top of him. At which time he gets up and runs around behind it, always on his back legs and pushes it another five feet which is maybe a mile in beetle space. Off he goes pushing it again, falls down another fifteen times, always jumps right back up, doesn't take time to cuss, no time for that, always packing it so it won't come apart. Then he comes to his hole and in the both of them go, disappeared. A little bit later out he comes again, flaps his conductor's wings and helicopters back to the farm. By then the whole cow plop is quivering and hundreds of beetles are rolling their prizes toward home."

I was still a little too surprised by Joshua to get into the spirit of his story. All I could say was, "Do you always talk this way to strangers?"

"Jinks told me about you."

"Told you what?"

"About mother and why she hired you."

"Why was that?"

"Her fears, dreams."

I asked, "What would you do if it was your job to protect a man who refused to be protected?"

"Probably what you're doing; discover what it is he needs to be protected from. I believe that if we can understand disasters in advance it is possible to avert them."

"That's what I'm trying to do." He and I looked at each other for a while and I shifted lines of thought. "You seem awfully reasonable regarding this danger to your father. Maybe you don't believe any of it."

"I wish that was the case, but I've seen Mother's dreams work too often. Once when I was about twenty, I walked into this room and sat down in that rocker over there and began reading a book in front of the fire. Mother was asleep on the couch and she didn't stir when I walked in. Outside it was dark and windy. I put more wood on the fire, then settled back to read Dostoevski's *The Eternal Husband.* Sometime later I was in the middle of a really intense passage, one that electrified my spine, when Mother became restless. I glanced up, thinking she was cold, but the fire was roaring and that wasn't it. I went back to the book. I remember I was shaking from the intensity of the passage when her restlessness increased and she jerked upright, awake. She gazed at me bewildered for a while, then began telling me of the nightmare she was having.

"In her nightmare she was holding a doorknob and listening intently as someone, some threat on the other side of the door listened to her while she listened. She went on telling me about the room she was in, the position of the furniture, the windows, antique lamps, and the hair was standing out on the back of my neck because she was describing, down to the minutest details, the scene I had been reading."

"Had she read the book?"

"Never heard of it."

"And you think this proves . . ."

"I'm not saying it proves anything. I'm only telling you my experience."

"Joshua," came an ancient woman's voice. "Where have you been?" A spry, wrinkled and white-haired woman, who, I guessed, was in her eighties, swept through the crowd toward us. Her face was carved into flat planes by the deep wrinkles, and the planes were crossed by smaller wrinkles, resembling the view of the desert from an airplane.

Joshua introduced me to Gracious Boulding as Jinks's boyfriend. Her glittering eyes swept from my face down and back up and said she more or less approved.

"Do you think he will last any longer than the others?"

"Maybe, Grandma."

"I wish she would have a child soon. That would cure her. I want another batch of grandchildren now that my precious ones are grown. When I was her age I was a pill, I tell you. You know that one song she does in Spanish on the record with the sexy picture of her on a mountaintop on the cover?"

"I like that song very much."

"I knew you'd remember that picture on the front. That song makes me cry so hard when I hear it. Listening to it I seem to see Arizona as it used to be when Dad Boulding and I would go to Tombstone for the Helldorado in our Model-A Ford. . . ." Talking about it apparently brought back the song and the memories because she suddenly began to weep happily and walked off toward the punch bowl, her spine erect.

Joshua didn't seem to feel at all that need some people have to apologize on behalf of emotional relatives. In the darkness outside, white-limbed trees bowed before rushing wind and snapped erect when the currents shifted.

Joshua tossed his head to one side, causing a series of popping noises in his neck, and be blinked violently. "Did you know the Chinese recently tested their bomb and the radioactivity is spreading over us in this wind right now?" he asked and walked away. He looked back at me over his shoulder, motioning me to follow.

We pushed through clusters of guests and went out the front door. The wind was so strong I had to use both hands to close the door gently.

"I try not to read the papers any more than I have to," I said.

I followed him across the yard into a dark corner where he urinated into a flower bed. "There might be some hope yet," he said. "An underground group recently dynamited a uranium mine in south France."

"That cloud," he said, pointing to one that was sliding in front of the moon. "Doesn't it look like a weasel?"

"More like a turtle to me."

"Good, you're an honest man. Tell me, do you ever see snakes?"

"In the desert—"

"I don't mean in the desert. Do you ever see snakes?"

"I'm not sure I know what you mean."

"Well, forget it." He walked back inside.

A waitress with a tray of drinks offered me one and I took it.

"What do you think of this reactor my father and uncle have all those contracts for?" he asked me.

"I don't know what to think yet."

"You realize, don't you, there's no such thing as the peaceful atom because there's no such thing as peaceful man. One man builds a house with a hammer, another kills with it. Tools are tools, nothing more."

"*Qué hubo le, Joshua?*" said one of the waiters who was standing just behind him. He put his hand on Joshua's shoulder.

"*Eh, Joaquin, qué tal?*"

"Hey, man, I wanted to tell your sister that every time I get too blue I listen to that song of hers about the moon. That song it makes Yolanda and me cry and then in bed afterwards, well . . . that Jinks, her voice can squeeze my heart. The rest of these *cabrón gringos*, they ruin the spirit of everything they touch. I better get back to work, man, this *pendejo* boss of mine, he told us you are all important *gente*, man, and we better not talk to you."

"When you're through work, I've got some beer in the car," said Joshua. "We can go drink it and help Chato doctor Jinks's filly."

"Maybe Jinks will sing again for her friends, eh? She still sing for her friends now she's a big shot?"

"Just give her a bottle of Ripple," said Joshua.

"I better go," said Joaquin. "My boss, he looked at me a couple times already." Joaquin went off through the crowd, carrying his tray of empty glasses.

A governor's aide had been standing near us. I figured he had been waiting for a chance to ingratiate himself with a Boulding and Joshua was the nearest. He touched his elbow.

"Have you heard what precautions the World Health Organization recently recommended be taken against fallout?" he asked Joshua. He also put a hand on my sore elbow, to welcome me into the conversation.

"Nope."

The governor's aide chuckled slightly with irrepressible mirth before he said, "Stick it back in and take shorter strokes. For fallout."

Several men around us, who had apparently been eavesdropping on our conversation, burst into laughter, and there was some actual knee slapping and coughing. When the laughter quieted, there were six of us standing in a circle. They were expecting our circle to be one where rousing good jokes were told. The governor's aide was beaming with pleasure and a sense of success as Joshua glared at him and said: "You got it wrong. You guys that can't tell a joke straight disgust me. You just told us about your own impotence. The real thing you do for fallout is wear a lead jockstrap."

There was a stunned silence, and Joshua walked away. The governor's aide coughed and sipped his drink. All the men around us were wearing adhesive labels on their lapels which gave their names and corporations: one from Hughes, one from American, one from Anaconda.

My face tightened into an emotionless mask as I noticed the last one who had joined us, the county attorney, recently elected. I had old scores to settle with him, and as one of the pretty young waitresses took his empty glass and replaced it with a full one, I said, "Miss, that empty glass you took from Mr. Skinner; don't wash it."

"Sir?"

"Break it. After where his lips have been, it cannot be cleaned."

"Sir?"

"After Les Skinner drinks from a glass, break it. You can have no idea where his lips have been."

Skinner glared at me, stung by my attack. He had a wide mustache and a small chin which made him look like a rodent.

"Who *is* this clown?" he asked the man to his right.

"Dan Falconer. I hear he and Miss Boulding go out together."

"Coyote turned gigolo, eh?" said Skinner.

# 7

I walked off smiling. Skinner's remark referred to work I had done for the previous county attorney, Matthew Gillette. In his campaign Matt had promised, if elected, to set up a list of priorities to calculate crime in terms of its real cost to society and to allocate his time and resources toward those most damaging, rather than the most dramatic, crimes.

Matt was a good speaker and he won the election, but when he actually started to turn the county attorney's office from an agency which primarily harassed the powerless to one that combated real crime, people were surprised. He kept his campaign promises, and segments of the business community were outraged. He soon got a tip that a local contractor was sending out trucks with four cubic yards of asphalt while the taxpayer was paying for five. Since he felt he could trust no one in the sheriff's department, he had deputized me and three other men. At eight-fifteen one morning we had made four simultaneous arrests: a truck driver (who turned state's evidence), the scale master at the asphalt company, the president of the asphalt company and the contractor who was building the road. Three convictions, and for the first time in Phoenix history the criminals who were making off with the big money went to jail. During the next few months in office the hot tips began to flow in as people's faith in Matt's honesty and his ability to do something grew.

Not long after that he had arrested and was prosecuting officials in a Blue Shield scandal, a state senator on a bribery charge, and many more contractors for "Short Work" of one kind or another. And there were many land fraud cases as well.

One of the main reasons for Matt's effectiveness was that he used me and three other old friends for his investigative work. We answered only to him; there were no leaks. We were known as Matt Gillette's Coyotes.

The other Coyotes and I were offered big money to leak Matt's plans, and one night, after I had turned down a bribe offer, Bandit woke me about three in the morning with his barking. I was crawling out my bedroom window with a gun in my hand toward where I heard Bandit growling and snapping and a man cussing. Then two shots. For a couple of minutes I thought they had killed my dog, but as I was loading my shotgun he appeared, shivering and angry, and the man had apparently left.

Five months before the next general election, Les Skinner had announced he would run against Matt. Out of nowhere hundreds of "Volunteers for Skinner" appeared to make phone calls and carry petitions from door to door. "Skinner for County Attorney" billboards appeared everywhere; enormous numbers of expensive television shorts told about the greatness of Les Skinner. One day I made notes and played around with my Japanese calculator and figured, roughly, that Skinner's campaign for county attorney cost more than most state governors spend on their campaigns. Matt Gillette's good work had raised a lot of money for Les Skinner.

About the same time an extensive smear campaign started against Matt in the Phoenix newspapers. It was well planned and it was ugly. He did nothing to counter it, figuring that doing his job well would speak for itself.

It didn't. The election was a rough day. Resolutions which essentially gave the green light to turning Arizona into Los Angeles East passed easily. Resolutions for nuclear safeguards were turned down as too expensive. And when the results of the election were in, Matthew Gillette had returned to private life.

"Honey," Jinks had come up to me. "Have you seen my father?"

"No," I said. "I thought you were going to find him."

"Well, I haven't yet and Grandma wants me to sing 'Happy Birthday' in Spanish, and the cook is ready to light the candles." She went off between the clusters of talkers, headed toward the punch bowl, standing on tiptoes and craning around searching for Cass. I scanned the crowd, looking for him, too. Then I saw Sheila Boulding back out of a conversation and turn to walk across the room. Her hands were clutched in front of her stomach and she seemed to be looking inward, listening intently, when she suddenly jerked as though some invisible fist had hit her in the back of the neck. Her head tossed back and her mouth flew open and she appeared to slip into some sort of trance. She was so far from me I couldn't have caught her if she fell, and I thought the dark-suited men around would turn to help her, but to those nearest her she seemed not to exist. They kept right on with the party conversation. Her knees seemed to buckle, but she brought herself out of it, shook herself, forged forward through the crowd and disappeared into a back room.

# 8

I stepped away from the crowd still looking for Boulding. I looked around, from one cluster of standing talkers to another, and I recognized many people I had investigated while working for Matt Gillette. I guessed that a good fifty percent of the Phoenix wealth was controlled or heavily influenced by the people in the room.

Many were legitimate businessmen or bureaucrats, so far as I knew, but many were not. Judge Frederick Blankenburg stood with a drink in his hand talking with great animation, his round jowls hopping like the hams of a running hog. The last time I'd seen him he was asleep in his robes, sitting behind his bench, his face spilling over the palm of the hand on which it rested. There was a murder trial in session, and Matt Gillette was prosecuting. The victim of the hit-man on trial had been shot the night before he was scheduled to testify in a land fraud case. Matt had just said that if witnesses can be murdered with impunity, our legal system will collapse, and Judge Blankenburg slept through it until Matt woke him with some sharp words, to which the judge said, "Are you addressing this court with contempt?" Matt answered, "I'm trying not to show it." A little later Blankenburg found a technical problem and threw the case out of court.

In another cluster of people I saw Jack Romulus, the man against whom the murdered witness was going to testify. Romulus and the murdered man had been partners in a land sales company which, among other things, sold remote canyons and gullies—land beautiful to look at but not good to build on—to servicemen overseas. After extensive investigation, I had discovered one choice four-acre parcel to which fifteen servicemen held title. Jack had paid $100 per acre for the land and had sold it for $4,000, then sold it another fourteen times for $4,000 just to make sure he wasn't cheating himself.

The case had been a difficult one involving high-level politicians and bureaucrats on the civilian side and brass on the military, and it didn't look like we were going to go anywhere with it till Romulus's partner decided to speak. The partner was murdered, and that seemed to perform lobotomies on the other sources the Coyotes and I had questioned. They didn't remember their own names after that.

Across the room I spotted an ex-sheriff who had resigned after I had presented Matt with clear evidence that the sheriff was the major stockholder in a string of massage parlors. We also found that heroin confiscated by his department one week turned up for sale on the streets three weeks later. By chemical analysis, the same batch.

Hovering near the door to the kitchen, looking about as relaxed as a white cop in a black neighborhood, was another old acquaintance. Ralph Stark was a little over six feet tall, and his nose was permanently flattened from one cheek to the other. I know, because I flattened it. Ralph was a city detective at the time he asked a personal friend of mine, a rape victim, if she enjoyed the crime. I found him that night, off duty, in a bar, and I taunted him until he threw the first punch, in front of witnesses.

"Are you always such a quiet man?" Gracious Boulding had appeared beside me. Her hair was white, and every few seconds she alternately smiled and frowned. Before I could answer she said, "Jinks needs a quiet man, or else you'd both be jabbering at the same time." She scrutinized my face, perhaps looking for signs of money, breeding or quality, as grandmothers do. "I suppose," she said, "you're better for her than those Hollywood types. She told me a little about them. My, the things you youngsters do to each other. What did you say you did for a living, Mr. . . . ." She grimaced an instant, searching for my name, then dismissed the problem. "I guess it doesn't much matter what you do. Jinks will make enough for the both of you, and for ten other families besides. Imagine, she used to go off into the desert and sing by herself when she was a little girl. I never guessed it would come to this. But you won't waste it, will you? You're not after her money, are you?" She fixed me with a threatening glare and took my measure. "You don't gamble, do you? Still, you should keep busy. Oh, hello, Judge," she said to Blankenburg, who had been beckoning to her with his eyes. She swept away from me to the judge's group.

In another group was a state congressman named Koppel, who had, according to my sources in Mexico, invested heavily in Sierra Madre land where poppies are grown. Many of his political and legal connections were helpful in importing the processed heroin north by plane from Mexico into the states.

A mountain-lion skin, with the snarling head intact, hung on the south wall. Next to the skin the Maricopa County real estate commissioner, George Pellissier, was gesturing emphatically about something. While working for Matt, I had been assigned to George for quite a while. When most officials take bribes, they ask what they are supposed to do *before* taking the money. Not George. He took the money first, then asked what he was supposed to do. He knew exactly what a public office was supposed to do—make him rich. In this he was as singleminded and accessible as a mongrel bitch in heat.

One of the last glimpses I'd had of George's political dealings had been through a telephoto lens. One hundred and fifty hundred-dollar bills were passing from George's hands into Les Skinner's. The two had met on a dirt road west of the city, and I was on a hill above them.

There were more men in that room whose secret public lives I knew more about than it was safe or pleasant to know. We Coyotes had done deep background investigative work on many public officials. We had fat files full of photographs, grand-jury testimonies and copies of falsified documents. We had so many arrests planned, Matt had to put them on a secret calendar to give himself time to assemble the evidence into good cases.

But then Matt Gillette lost the election.

I was thinking maybe I would take a vacation after all when I spotted Joshua near the fireplace. I walked across the room to talk to him some more.

# 9

A mariachi band of six strolled along singing requests. I slid past several groups of people toward the fireplace where Joshua was on his knees placing large logs on a roaring fire. One log knocked a shower of sparks, spreading throughout the enormous fireplace and rising slowly up the chimney. In between the notes of the mariachi singers the wind howled outside, and white branches flashed past the darkened windows.

"Is something wrong with your mother? She wasn't looking well a few minutes ago."

"You name it," Joshua said, ending that conversation with his tone.

I looked into the flames for a while until I said, "I love a mesquite fire. Whenever I get to feeling bad I go off into the desert and build a fire and stare into it all night."

"What do you see?"

"Whatever has been hiding from me in the city."

His eyes narrowed as he watched me closely and said, "Here, look at this."

He pointed with his toe to the bare footprint of a tiny child embossed in the cement hearth. By the look on his face I could tell it was his footprint. "There you have my secret," he said. "This fireplace was once big as a cave to me, these beamed ceilings high as a cathedral vault, and the desert outside was a giant mystical world. Out my bedroom window I once saw a mountain lion, which was bigger to me and filled with more significance than any African lion could have been. And on my father's land I've seen eagles and wolves and bobcats. And now they're dead. Arizona is being Californicated, and my relatives are the sperm."

"How do you live with yourself?"

"Maybe you noticed I'm drinking water. I no longer drink or eat from profits I don't respect. My father in his later years has begun to understand what he's destroying, but Claude is absolutely impervious to any form of thinking that doesn't involve property, much more property than he can ever use in any sane way. But what more can I do, I ask you? I can't kill him."

"Joshua, have you seen Dad?" asked Jinks, coming up to us. She was worried.

He said no and she sighed and went off again. The lead singer in the mariachi band tossed his head questioningly at her, and when she shrugged her shoulders they began to sing "Rancho Grande" one more time than it ought to be sung in any one evening. The cook leaned in from the kitchen and waved a question toward her, but she had no answers for him either.

I saw Sheila Boulding, standing by herself off in a corner. Her face was drained of color and she looked exhausted.

I nudged Joshua. "Your mother—over there—she really doesn't seem to be feeling well tonight."

"Festive occasions remind her of what she didn't do with her life," replied Joshua. Somewhere a door slammed.

"Festive occasions like this? Your father is an important man. And it seems he has a lot of important friends," I said with an ironic note so carefully tucked away in my voice that Joshua could hear it or ignore it as he chose.

"Friends? Jinks and I are his only *friends* here. Maybe Chato, too. But he says he has one other. Someone he hasn't known very long who talked truth to him. Dad mentioned him once without saying his name. Said he is one fine person."

Across the room I saw Cass Boulding enter by the kitchen door. Joaquin slid past him, carrying a tray of glasses, and Jinks walked up to him without showing the least elation that he had finally arrived. She asked him a question, he shook his head no, and she walked away.

"Your father's arrived," I said to Joshua.

He gave a quick glance over his shoulder, grunted and went back to poking the fire.

Then Cass looked directly at me and I expected some signs of displeasure on his face. The previous day he'd told me he never wanted to see me again, and here I was in the middle of his birthday party talking to his son.

But he showed no displeasure. Nor any recognition.

Jinks passed by again, muttering to herself, "Goddam inconsiderate son-of-a-bitch."

Joshua caught the perplexed look on my face and said, "You're not the first one to mistake the two of them."

There was a deep and ironic bitterness in his voice, and I suddenly remembered the other brother of Boulding Brothers Construction. When I'd been investigating the company for Matt, Claude Boulding had been away running the Las Vegas branch of the company and I had never seen him, nor a picture of him, before.

Now that I knew I wasn't looking at Cass, small differences in appearance emerged, even at that distance. Still, there was an amazing resemblance. Strong Boulding genes.

"Are they twins?" I asked.

"They sure look it," Joshua snapped. I realized I could grow tired of him very quickly.

"Is it Claude's birthday, too?"

More sparks rose up the chimney. "No," he said.

Jinks came back. "That governor's aide said he thought he saw him about an hour ago," she mumbled. "But no one else has."

I asked, "Did Chato change his mind about coming to the party? Maybe he would—"

"That's a thought," Joshua said to me. "He might be talking to Chato. Your filly caught a cold in this wind and Chato set up a cot next to her stall in the barn. Dad could be talking to him and have forgotten all about this."

"I'll go look," I said, feeling a surprising surge of usefulness. I don't like getting paid for nothing.

"Josh, you better go, too. Dad won't like it if Daniel goes alone."

Outside, as we walked toward the barn, thick clouds were sliding low overhead and flying sand stung my face. Somewhere a piece of loose barn tin creaked. A Doberman, perhaps the brother of the one I had left on top of the hill above Cass Boulding's second house, came up growling.

"You get along with that dog?" I asked.

"Sure. I played with him when he was a pup."

"Yeah. Well, he doesn't seem friendly to me."

"Don't worry," Joshua said.

Chato was rubbing the filly when we entered. Mucus had built up in her nose and she was wheezing heavily. The noise from the flapping tin was louder now that we were inside.

"She going to make it?" asked Joshua.

"You bet'cha," said Chato. False confidence, it seemed to me.

Joshua asked if he'd seen Cass. Chato didn't look away from the shining horse hair as he said he hadn't seen Cass in the last day or so. That was no help.

Back in the house the band was playing "Rancho Grande" once more. The instruments were badly tuned. We went through the kitchen into an office and told Jinks the news from Chato. She said she'd better try to call the trailer at the construction site. She was biting the inside of her lip furiously as she mumbled, "Goddam, I've got a burr up my ass the size of Texas."

Joshua said he'd look around once more and left the room. After a few minutes it became clear that Cass was not going to answer the trailer phone, so Jinks called the guardhouse at the gate to the entrance. The guard said he didn't know a thing.

Joshua came back saying he had spoken to the governor's aide who said he had seen Cass an hour earlier at the party. He had seen him across the room wearing a tan corduroy suit. Jinks rubbed her face and said her father didn't own a tan corduroy suit. Then she called the guards back to ask them to go to the construction trailer and see if Cass's car was there.

After she hung up she said, "But that's no answer. He often leaves his car there and rides home with Uncle Claude. Or he drives a company truck."

"Right now anything will help," said Joshua, and left the room again.

A minute later the phone rang and the guard told her Cass's car was outside the Boulding trailer and that lights were on inside but that there was no sign of Cass anywhere.

"Will you please go look around for him?" she said to the guard. "He sometimes goes for walks in the desert to think. Or you might look around the plant itself. Sometimes he goes to inspect work when the mood hits him."

She hung up and Joshua came back in to report that Claude said he hadn't seen Cass since late afternoon at the job.

# 10

Sheila Boulding came to join us in the office. Joshua had told her the results of our search and her face was still bloodless.

"We can't find him anywhere, Mother," Jinks said.

"I've got a feeling," said Sheila, more to herself than to the rest of us. She massaged the back of her neck and closed her eyes.

Joshua sat on the edge of a large maple desk and asked, "Have you tried his other house yet?"

I asked for the number and dialed it. There was no answer.

Then Gracious Boulding swept into the room. "Have you found him?" Her innumerable wrinkles were all shaped by dread.

Jinks said, "We're worrying for nothing, perhaps. He probably ran into some hard problem with the plant and walked off into the desert to think. You know how he is."

Gracious whirled and took my hand between hers and

squeezed. "You know where he is, don't you?"

"Not yet."

"This man, he's our hope, our only hope. You will find him, won't you. You will, won't you?" Gracious demanded.

I patted her hand, "So far he's only late to his birthday party. I'm not sure what's happening yet."

"He's our hope. You're our only hope. You're a good man. I can see it in your eyes. You're a smart man. When Cass was a little boy—this was all desert and pasture then—I used to wait for him to come home from school. Sometimes he was late like this and I used to worry myself sick. I'd say, *'Now, Cass, don't go too far'* when he'd go out to play. And one night he didn't come home at all and Dad Boulding brought in men and a Yaqui Indian to track him (oh, it was Chato's father; I forget his name but it was Chato's father) and there were men on horseback with flashlights everywhere in the mountains behind the house. And at dawn the next morning Chato's father found Cass asleep in a cave."

"There you go," I said, "there was nothing to worry about."

Gracious's eyes brightened and she squeezed my hand. "Go look in that cave," she said.

"I'll check out every possibility."

By the changed look on Gracious's face I thought she caught the concern for her sanity in my voice, and mistook it for condescension. She let go of my hand and turned to her son. "This son-of-a-bitch doesn't believe me. Claude, you go look in that cave."

"I was a little boy then, Mother. I don't know which one you mean."

"Oh, you're worthless, too," she said. "Joshua, go get Chato and tell him to find his father. Quick. I mean it."

"His father's dead, Grandma."

"You're worthless like your uncle."

"No, I'm not worthless, Grandma. You're just upset." Joshua put his arms around Gracious and calmed her enough so that she was silent.

Jinks and I traded conspiratorial glances when I said I wanted to drive over to the construction site and have a look around. She said she would go with me.

We went out the back door to avoid explanations to the guests, and as we were walking up the road between the lines of cars toward my truck, I said, "Your grandmother's opinion of me went through some pretty swift and violent changes."

"That was nothing," she said. "Gracious always has someone who's *the most*, and someone who is *worthless*, and her categories can swap without a moment's notice. Joshua and I used to wake up in the morning wondering which of us was going to be an angel and which the devil for that day."

"That must have been confusing."

"It was, until we were old enough to realize she's crazy. It must have been worse for Dad and Uncle Claude, because she was younger then and it was not yet clear that the angels and the devils were inside her."

# 11

The cyclone fencing around the entrance to the construction site was locked. Jinks shook it and shouted into the windy darkness beyond, but there was no response. Finally I suggested we force our way into the guardhouse next to the gate and find a phone there to call back to other numbers on the guard circuit.

Jinks entered the guardhouse, turned on the light and gasped. Only one of the two night guards was there, lying on a small mattress in the corner of the small room. His head was turned toward the wall and his right arm rested on a pile of pulp magazines.

The sound of Jink's sharp intake of air roused the guard out of a deep sleep. He raised his head, was irritated, blinked heavily to adjust to the sudden light.

"Look, I tell you, Miss Boulding, we walked all over this place looking for your father. We left the Boulding trailer just like it was, in case he might be around here and come back. The car he sometimes drives is in front."

We had entered the construction site through the back gate of the guardhouse. Now we decided to look at the Boulding trailer ourselves. It was quite a hike to it and dust whipped by the wind stung our faces. To our left the gaunt ironwork skeleton of the nuclear power plant rose up, framed against the night sky by the strings of naked light bulbs.

When we got to the construction trailer Jinks opened it with a key her father had given her. I went straight to his desk and looked under it. All I found was an old pair of dust-covered boots that looked like Cass had walked a thousand miles in them.

Jinks saw the question in my face and said, "He likes to work barefoot. He usually comes in from the job, puts his boots where you see them and does paper work for a while. Then, if he needs to clean up, he goes in there and takes a shower and dresses. He keeps clothes here for that reason." She opened a closet door to show me hanging clothes and a small chest of drawers full of socks and underwear. On the floor was a large mound of dirty work clothes.

"Who was your father talking to yesterday when we came to visit him here?"

"I don't know."

"It sounded like the other man wanted Cass to be a peacemaker of some sort, but your father said the other man was lucky he hadn't killed him. Does Cass always indulge in loose talk like that? Empty threats about killing and so on?"

"Not around me he doesn't. No, I don't think so. He's not like that," Jinks said.

Jinks browsed through the closet a minute. "His best suit and shoes aren't here. He must have come in from the job, done some paper work, showered, dressed and..."

From the mound of dirty clothes I picked up the shirt I had seen him wearing through the binoculars. It was still damp with perspiration.

"I can smell him," she said. "I really love his smell. Oh, and he's wearing his good-luck charm." She pointed to an empty nail in the side of the closet. "An Apache beadwork pouch. He always wears it under his shirt. The design on it represents the sun giving life to the earth. Chato's father gave it to him."

I went back to his desk and tried the drawers. They were locked. There was one drawer large enough to contain at least one of the briefcases I had seen and I gave it a quick jerk to see if the lock would force easily. It didn't. Then a light flashed in the corner of my vision.

Motioning for Jinks to come over next to me, I pointed to the lighted button on the telephone.

"Number six. It's the guardhouse," she said.

"Why didn't it ring?"

"It only rings when this number is dialed."

"Pick it up."

"They'll hear it click."

"That's all right. Try to recognize the voice."

She picked it up and listened for a moment before she said into the receiver, "Sorry, I pushed the wrong button. I was trying to call out." Then she pushed another button and left the receiver off the hook for a moment.

"It was the guard talking," she said. "He had just asked

someone what to do about you and me, but the other person didn't answer."

I went into the blueprint room and searched till I found a stainless-steel ruler, returned and placed it in the crack between the drawers and said, "You break the lock. There might be something in there we need to see and Les Skinner will lock me up for ten years if I break it."

"Dad's walnut desk?"

"He'll thank you. Hurry."

The wood snapped and the empty drawer slid open. Then I remembered what a burglar once told me about a safe place to hide valuables. I went back to the open closet and began digging down through the pile of ammonia-smelling work clothes. Underneath it all was the small gray briefcase I had seen Cass Boulding carrying just before his Doberman had caught my scent.

I brought it back to the desk and told Jinks to break it open while I held it on the table. The briefcase was the kind advertised by dropping it from an airplane at five thousand feet, and it took some real work with the heel of my shoes and the ruler to open it.

Finally the lock broke. The suitcase was packed full of fat manila envelopes, addressed and stamped. There were unmailed letters to the Los Angeles *Times*, the New York *Times*, and the Washington *Post*. I'd only had time to read three addresses when I heard a man's voice and looked up.

The guard walked across the room and took the lid of the briefcase and closed it firmly on my left hand. My right hand was at my side, and I did not follow my first—

and maybe worst—impulse. The guard had a pistol on his hip. He raised the briefcase lid enough for me to remove my left hand.

"I'm sorry, Miss Boulding. You'll have to go," he said.

"Dad asked me to bring this to him," she said, and glared at the guard with a look that I thought would have withered any man not acting on orders.

"You'll have to go," he repeated, and taking the briefcase with him, backed away in case I decided to fight him for it. But I knew better. One fist to his face would put me in jail for two years with Les Skinner prosecuting and Blankenburg presiding.

# 12

The roller coaster road rose and fell beneath my truck. Beside me Jinks held my arm and watched while my headlights sliced up and down through the darkness. Her face was clouded both with fears remembered and fears of the future. To ease her concern I tried to make small talk.

"I liked your last record," I said. "You wrote most of your own songs, didn't you?"

"All of them," said one fragment of her attention, harshly.

"I'm sorry. I didn't mean—"

"Don't worry. I wasn't short with you because of . . . I often do songs I haven't written. But I wrote all of those."

She fell silent but still stared at the side of my face. The ups and downs of the two-lane road were caused by the arroyos running down from the desert mountains which were silhouetted against the dark sky on our left. I had to drive carefully. Gusts of wind kept nudging the truck from one side to the other and I continually had to compensate.

"What do you do, Daniel?" There was desperation in her voice. She had broken out of her fear enough to try to divert herself by talking about me. "I know about your work with Matt Gillette, but what did you do before that?"

"Projects," I said. "I do projects. A few years ago I made a film of the Seri Indians in Mexico. I wanted to use it to get a reservation for them before they are destroyed by the Mexican government and the *gringo touri*. Another project was to discourage a ring of bighorn sheep and mountain-lion poachers I discovered in Phoenix."

"How did you do that?"

"I was forced to destroy four pickup trucks and a helicopter one night."

"How do you make a living doing things like that?"

"I don't need much, and other projects I've done paid me a little."

"You're a modern Don Quixote, always doing what is honorable," she said, grinning.

"Let's hope I'm not as blind."

I turned left, onto the road leading to Cass Boulding's second house. We ascended a ridge. In the distance to our right the city lay spread out, twinkling beneath a cloud of dust.

"Who's Homer?" I asked. "Joshua's friend? He said he was hiking in the mountains with Homer the other day."

She laughed at me, then said, "Josh reads a lot. Whoever he's reading is his friend."

"He seems a little crazy, that brother of yours. You've got quite a family."

"You would be, too, if . . . he spent two years in the jungle as a medic. For seven hundred days he saw at least two violent deaths a day and had to zip them into body bags himself. The marines gave him a permanent medical pension, but he won't take it. I've handed him money, but he drops it at my feet. All he does is hike through mountains and read."

"How does he eat?"

"Oh, I think he steals chickens. Once I had dinner with him and Joaquin and other friends in the desert, and Josh was plucking chickens. When he gets real sick and stays drunk, Chato's family takes him in, or Joaquin's. When that happens I give Melba money to cover his groceries. If you ever tell Joshua that, I'll never speak to you again."

"I'll keep it to myself."

"Even before his military experience he was having a bad time of it. He once told me that he had one dream many times. He would be in love with a beautiful woman. . . . He said they were long dreams, this loving part. Then they would start to make love, and he would have his arms around her, would be kissing her, and he would look into her eyes and her eyes would vanish. There would be nothing but two holes where her eyes had been, and he would look through those holes and inside would be a hideous creature of some sort. . . . He would tear himself loose and run and she would chase him and he would wake up screaming."

"Sounds like nights were pretty busy times on the Boulding ranch. Lots of bad dreams."

"Once last year I came back to my apartment and found him asleep in my flower bed. He was drunk and it was raining, and when I woke him up, he looked so earnestly at me, and with such pity said, 'Joe was cutting off their ears.' I think he was talking about Joe Lopez, who joined the marines with him. I asked him if it was, but he wouldn't talk about it once he was awake."

We came to a cattle guard set in cement with a metal gate locked across the road. The lock was too big to break and too hardened to saw, so Jinks suggested we park my truck and walk in. She said she thought it wasn't much more than a mile to the house, and I didn't tell her that I knew exactly how far it was because I had hiked it ten hours earlier. The teeth holes beneath the bandage on my forearm were suddenly aching, and I put my pistol in my belt.

We left the road and took a shortcut. Jinks told me she had never been to Cass's second ranch before because he only allowed Chato to visit. But she knew right where she was going. She said she had ridden this land on horseback when she was in her teens, and she headed straight toward the ridge overlooking the house, to the place where I had killed the Doberman. Not wanting her to find it, I sped up and veered off to the left, signaling her to follow, but she went her own way. I was a good hundred yards away from her, in an arroyo, when I heard her cry out.

I was sure what it was but took my pistol out of my belt so that I would seem more surprised. I was coming up out of the arroyo, passing beneath the one large mesquite in the area, when the tree exploded. I raised my hand and nearly fired before my head cleared enough to see the black branches leaping away to swoop and glide and flap heavily through the windy night. I had stumbled into a buzzard's roost and the sky around me was black with wheezing wings.

When I reached Jinks she was bending over the Doberman's hollow-eyed head, picking up his rabies tag from the dark ground. I shined a light on them for her. A hundred yards to one side of us a coyote yapped and on the other side another coyote answered.

"Someone shot Pete," she said. "Someone killed Dad's watchdog." In her voice I could hear her worries about Cass linking to the dead dog, and I wanted to tell her what happened. But I was thinking, *Something is going on here and I'm not showing any of my cards until I find out what it is.*

Jinks beat at the door as if she meant to break it. There was a Boulding Brothers truck parked outside, and it seemed possible that Cass would open the door, and ask Jinks what was the matter.

But he didn't. Nor did anyone else. Before I knew it, Jinks had raised a long leg and gracefully kicked in a window and reached in to unlock the door from the inside. I motioned to her to follow me, and since the house was laid out roughly as the family house had been, I pretty well knew the way as I went through turning on lights, until I came to her father's office. Then I stopped in the doorway. She was close behind me.

"This is eerie," she said, looking past me into a hard-wood-paneled office. "It's exactly like the one at home. Everything is."

I went in and moved slowly through the room. Behind his desk, on the floor, was a sheepskin coat and a rain parka in a heap. Beneath the heap were the two large briefcases. There was no lock on them. I opened one and took out a cassette tape, held it up and shrugged a question at Jinks.

"They're all over. When he thinks about a problem, he dictates to himself," she said. "Like some people keep a diary, he clarifies his thoughts by talking."

I saw then that there were several cassette tapes in front of me on the desk. I wondered what was in them. I picked one at random marked December 12 and plugged it in. Cass Boulding's voice said: *"Every time Congress considers an alternative to nuclear energy, the response is that it is too costly. Every time nuclear energy is questioned, the one asking the questions is accused of wanting to destroy jobs."*

I thought whoever had called the guard at the construction site might be following us, so I knew I didn't have much time to listen to many of the cassettes in the briefcases. But I pulled out one tape and put in another, listening to Cass Boulding's voice for the next few minutes.

*"This blind faith that science will solve all problems it causes is unscientific. . . .*

*"Listening to those two sheep engineers talk was like listening to two suicides arguing about which poison is better. . . .*

*". . . It is like introducing bacteria from Mars . . . something never before in the environment . . . the world has discovered its Ice-Nine. . . ."*

"Do you have any idea what is going on?" I asked Jinks.

"None," she said, her face weary and afraid.

"Do you know what he meant yesterday when he poked himself in the chest and told you he had the answers there? When he said that you should stay out of his way?"

"I thought it probably had something to do with our family."

"So did I—at the time. But I wonder if it did."

I decided to take a chance and asked: "I think your father and Chato had some sort of secret project. Do you know what it was?"

"No."

"Do you trust me?" I asked.

"No," she said again, and began to weep.

"Will you do yourself a favor and authorize me to take these tapes and any papers we can find to your apartment for safekeeping? If anything has happened, any information I can get my hands on will be helpful."

When I replaced the cassettes and picked up the briefcases I felt why Chato had stooped with their weight. The trees were waving like grass in the wind, as I went out of the yard and down into an arroyo to the south of the house and stashed the briefcases beneath a mesquite. I wanted to examine the barn, and if someone came in on us while we were there, I wanted to be able to sneak back later for the diaries.

Jinks spoke to Cass's remaining dogs, explaining to them that she wanted me to break into the barn, while I found a piece of pipe to use as a pry bar.

Once inside the barn I turned on the lights. By then I was so jumpy I had my gun in my hand, and I nearly shot a barn cat as it streaked in front of me. Pigeons flapped among the rafters. Gradually I calmed enough to see that the barn I was in the middle of was large, well lit and remarkably clean.

In one corner there was a tack area where saddles were slung over sawhorses and bridles hung from the wall. There were a few ranch tools, shovels, post-hole diggers and fence pliers, but the whole lot of it would have fit in the back of my truck. So why a barn large enough for a gymnasium?

The only thing of any size was a pile of barley bags stacked about twelve feet high in the southeast corner. I did a quick computation in my head and came up with enough barley to last three horses seven years, give or take three. There were a lot of oats.

I felt somehow that what had gone into those three briefcases had originated in this barn and somewhere there was at least a tape recorder.

Taking my knife I went over to the stacked barley bags and stabbed one. Sand slid between the parted burlap into my hands.

Jinks took a pinch of sand from my palm and said, "I don't like this."

"Neither do horses," I said, and I wondered about the bags. Were they a barrier, hiding something? Cautiously, I began to climb the sandbags until I stood on the top one.

The bags didn't go all the way to the wall, as they appeared to. There was only one row of them, a false front, and behind them was a room. I didn't have to climb down the bags on that side, because there was an aluminum ladder.

The doorless room behind the bags turned out to be an office. There were drafting lamps such as those found in the construction trailer, table space, a dictaphone, a typewriter, a Xerox photocopy machine and a microfilming machine like the ones I sometimes used while doing land title research for Matt Gillette.

I calculated the cost of the equipment in this secret office at about fifty thousand dollars, but there was not one piece of information in it. Not one piece of microfilm, not one piece of paper or photocopy, not one cassette tape.

I guessed that he must have finished whatever work he was doing and had loaded the results into the two large briefcases and the one small one and had then abandoned his secret bunker.

Jinks had climbed up, and now she stood on the top of the sandbags near the top of the ladder, looking down at me. "I don't like the looks of all this," she said. "What's it all about?"

"Let's get out of here," I said, and I climbed the ladder, heaved myself over the top sandbag and we climbed down the other side.

The wind had died down and the air was cold. Ahead of us the lights of Phoenix stretched across the floor of the desert.

As we approached the truck, I was jolted again when another large mesquite tree defoliated. The buzzards I had scared out of their roost earlier had come down to rest here. They flapped heavily through the dark air. Their wings sounded like labored breathing and around us the coyotes howled.

I heaved the briefcases into the front seat of my truck, made a U-turn and headed back toward the city. Again the up and down over the roller coaster road, the headlights rising and falling until Jinks asked me to pull over to the side of the road and stop.

She put her arms around my neck and hugged me, but her head was averted. She didn't want my lips; she wanted the curve my neck made with my shoulder, a warm, enclosed place. She said softly, "I'm sorry I said I didn't trust you. What I mean, I don't trust anyone now, I don't trust any man. Except Joshua, I suppose. But I don't mistrust you. I have seen no reason for mistrusting you. Do you understand?"

"I think so," I said. I had my arm around her to comfort her, and I was looking over her shoulder, out the back window of my truck and into the front window of my camper shell. There, in the glimmering light from my dashboard reflecting through the parallel panes of glass, I saw a man's shoe. For a while I tried to remember if it was my shoe, but as I looked at it, my eyes adjusted to the absence of light behind us and I saw that there was a leg connected to the shoe. Gradually a form began to emerge out of the tools and belongings I always carry in the back of the truck: gas cans, water cans, backpacks, toolboxes, spare tires and a Coleman lantern. I guessed that Cass Boulding was lying behind us.

I didn't breathe heavily, I thought, or tense one muscle

in response to what I saw, but my blood pressure shot up so fast my ears hissed and Jinks, still hugging me, sensed something. She asked: "What's the matter, Don Quixote?"

"I was just thinking we'd better get going," I said as I started the engine.

# 13

While we drove to her apartment, neither Jinks nor I spoke. My head was like a disturbed hornets' nest; thoughts flying everywhere. Most of the thoughts didn't make sense. I remembered an article about the governor of Wyoming around 1900 who'd cut down a lynched murderer and skinned him and made a leather jacket...I remembered fragments of old tunes...I heard that hissing of my blood through the canals of my inner ears.

Gradually more coherent thoughts began to surface through the wreckage. Cass Boulding's body was really in the back of my truck. Had it been put there while Jinks and I were examining his bunker? Had it been there during his own birthday party? Had it been in there all afternoon when my truck was parked in front of my house? Yesterday I had deposited my paycheck from Sheila Boulding. It would look so neat in the newspapers.

Les Skinner would be grinning in the front row as they strapped the Coyote into the chair.

I was going to have to hire Matt Gillette as my attorney.

Finally my thoughts came together as I stopped in front of Jinks's apartment and carried the two briefcases inside.

I felt with an intuitive certainty that half the people at Cass Boulding's party were connected to his death in one way or another. Some of them probably had been part of it without even knowing it, and all of them except Joshua and Jinks and Joaquin would be only too glad to solve Cass Boulding's murder by having the state murder me. And Les Skinner would be delighted to further discredit Matt Gillette by convicting me of murder.

The moment Cass Boulding's body and I were connected in any way, I would be arrested and I didn't want that. Coyotes are miserable in captivity.

"You know what I think, Don Quixote?" Jinks asked when we were in her apartment. "I think he might have run off with some woman to celebrate his birthday. That's what I think."

I wanted to tell her that her hopes were in vain, but I thought telling her that her father was dead would be like telling the world. Because of her fame, by morning the newspapers would be swarming on her like the buzzards on Pete's body for her reaction to her father's disappearance. If she knew he was dead she would act like he was dead—there was too much passion and vitality in her not to show her grief. If she thought he was alive, her hope would keep her moving ahead, she would act like a daughter waiting for her missing father. It might be cruel not to tell her right away, but I thought I'd better not.

I stood on her front porch, trying to leave, but I could tell from the look on her face that she didn't want to be left alone.

"Why don't you stay and we can listen to some more of his diary?" she asked.

"In the morning. I'm tired now."

"You know, I have the feeling he might call any time," she said.

"Good."

"If he does, I'll call you at home."

"Good idea."

"I don't want you to worry."

"Good."

"Does it matter what time? I don't want to wake you if he should call in the middle of the night."

"Any time, fine." I wasn't enjoying the conversation.

"You want some hot milk? Whenever I get too wound up to sleep, I drink hot milk."

"Good. None for me, thanks. I gotta go. I really do."

Back in my truck I could think more clearly. First, I needed to know whether I was being watched. There was no doubt that I had been set up; the question now was when they were going to arrest me. I drove out into the desert on Miraflores Road and kept watching my mirrors. No lights. I wasn't being followed. That I could see.

I turned right on Superstition Trail and headed toward the mountains. The winds buffeted my truck and I was still trying to clear my head. The thought that maybe I was mistaken about the shoe and Cass Boulding flashed across my mind. Maybe it had all been a dream. I laughed. That was it. I'd imagined it. I shook my head and decided to go home and forget about it. Then I told myself I had no time to be so crazy as I snatched a flashlight from my glove box and shined it over my shoulder.

Cass Boulding was lying exactly as I had seen him in the dark. He was faceup with his head behind my back and his feet near the tailgate. A front tire went off the pavement and I whirled around in time to right the truck on the road and began to realize that I would have to get rid of Cass's body soon.

But I had already known that. That's why I was driving east on Superstition Trail toward the mountains. Since the turn of the century nearly three hundred bodies have been found in the Superstitions. It had become an unofficial dumping ground.

Why was I reacting as though *I* had murdered Cass Boulding? Why wasn't I driving with Jinks to deliver her father to the police?

The answers crowded around me and they centered around the realization that whoever had placed the body in my truck must have planned for me to turn it in.

I came to a dirt road off to the right and had nearly driven onto it when I realized I had to stay on pavement. My tire tracks. When the body was discovered, tire tracks in the area would be photographed and compared to mine ...

Stay on pavement with the truck. Carry Cass Boulding

away from road into desert. Find a rocky area to avoid footprints.

Several miles later I came to a place where an arroyo had been crossed using large dynamited boulders for the roadbed. I stopped the truck and checked both front and back. There were no cars on the Superstition Trail as far as I could see.

I went around the the back of the truck and looked at the door on my camper shell. I had left it unlocked, so there was no possible defense stating that the lock had been busted. I threw open the door and shined the light on Cass Boulding's face, which was tilted up, his head pillowed by my toolbox. A thin black line of dried blood was across his lips and his nostrils. His eyes were closed.

I pulled him toward me by his ankles until I could get my arms under his armpits and lift. His head fell back terribly, as though it was hooked to his shoulders by only a string. I propped him up and lifted his head and examined his neck with the flashlight. It had been broken, I guessed, smashed by one blow from something blunt and heavy.

Realizing I had no time to examine him further, I held him up with one arm and closed the back of the truck and carried him to the side of the road. At the point where the pavement ended the rocks began, so I was leaving no tracks as I carried him over the edge of the road and started down the rock-strewn embankment. I was holding my small flashlight in my mouth and searching for footholds when the headlights of a car suddenly flashed to my left, beyond the front of my truck.

I rested my burden quickly to turn off my flashlight,

then picked him up and plunged on down the rocky embankment, carrying him off to one side, like a mother carries a three-year-old on a thrust hip. The first four blind, crashing steps I made all right, but the next rock I hit gave way and we began to roll, Cass Boulding and I, over and over with me on top of him and then him on top of me, with his head flying around, cracking against my skull and then flying away with each revolution.

Finally we were in deep sand at the bottom of the arroyo. Cass lay facedown beneath me, his head tucked unnaturally against his chest. The headlights from the car that had startled me were flooding the air above.

I was prepared to wait until they went past. Certainly they would go past. But they didn't pass. As the sound of the car and the funnel of lights in the air above slowed, I began to realize they were going to stop. I saw I was lying near a metal culvert and I rose up, lifted Cass Boulding by the back of his pants and shirt collar, pushed him into the culvert and then pushed on his feet until they were out of sight to anyone looking down from the road above.

Even before the car had stopped, a searchlight was passing over the surrounding desert and I could hear the raucous deep sound of a police radio in the background. The car came to a complete stop. The engine idled while the searchlight combed the desert, first to the west of the road, which I could see at the end of the tunnel, then to the east side. Because of the sharp angle of the side of the road, the searchlight would only reach within a hundred feet of where I was crouching in the mouth of the culvert.

The car door opened and there were footsteps across the pavement and the smaller beam of a flashlight zigzagging across the desert floor. I heard a snap as he unclasped the strap on his pistol.

"Anybody down there?" came an official voice in a guarded tone.

"Just us, sir," I said, raising my voice slightly into the falsetto of obedience.

"Who's us?"

"Me and Janie," I said. "You scared us."

He stood on the embankment next to my pickup, shining the light down on my right shoulder and leg, which was all of me that stuck out of the culvert.

"Aren't you and Janie cold?" he asked. As I hoped, he assumed I had undressed Janie, and he was going to make the most of the situation.

"No, sir."

"How do you keep from getting cold on a night like this, with the air freezing and the wind blowing?"

"We do all right. We're doing all right."

"And what are you doing?" He was nearly choking with mirth.

"We're watching the stars, sir."

"Can Janie see the stars from in there?"

"Janie? She's very frightened. You are frightening her. Weren't you ever young?"

"I still am," he said, and fell silent.

His footsteps crunched in the loose gravel covering the edge of the pavement, then were more solid as he walked around my truck. His flashlight beam searched this way and that in the truck. After a while he walked back to the edge and shined his light down on my shoulder once again.

"Do you realize you are illegally blocking a state highway and that I could ticket you for that?" he asked.

"No, sir; there wasn't much traffic and I thought . . . no, I guess I didn't think. I just got off a ship in San Diego and me and Janie haven't been together for a long time and I guess I didn't think . . ."

He was wheezing, suppressing a laugh. He said, "And what you're doing or about to do is also illegal."

"Sir, you're making Janie cry," I said.

Suppressing his laughter, he wheezed for a while before he said, "All right. I'll forget about it this time, but as soon as I leave I want you two to scramble up here and get that truck off the road. Get off on one of these dirt roads. On the double, sailor!" he said and burst out laughing, returned to his car and started to drive away. Then he stopped again and called out his window, "I'll be back in about ten minutes and I want you out of here."

When his headlights had disappeared I pulled Boulding's body out of the culvert by an ankle and threw all two hundred pounds of him over my shoulder like a sack of grain and ran up the sliding rocks to my truck.

# 14

Every imaginable impulse passed through me during the next hour. Should I drive to the police department and turn myself in; then depend on Sheila's money to get me out? Unless she was part of my setup. Should I go to Mexico? Should I stop and try to dig a grave alongside the road with my hands? No, the coyotes would dig him up if I did. I kept thinking about the governor of Wyoming actually skinning and tanning the hide of a human being, and I thought about coyotes.

I was thinking about it all so hard I didn't realize where I was until I was a good eighty miles northeast of Phoenix. Soon I recognized the highway and that I was driving sensibly—when an oncoming car dimmed its headlights on the two-lane, and I dimmed mine. I checked the gas. I had enough. I asked myself why I was eighty miles northeast of Phoenix and my mind answered with a picture of an open well.

It had been dug straight down through solid rock by

hand and dynamite during the 1930s. It was five-foot square and about sixty feet deep. The rancher who no longer used it had covered it with railroad ties but some hunters had uncovered it. I had found it once on a weekend campout and I had looked down at the glistening black water framed by the bottom of the shaft.

I found the turnoff and drove the six miles over the jeep trail. Yellow eyes of coyotes peered at me from the darkness and seemed to know more than I knew.

The desert around the well was empty. I lifted Cass out of the back of the truck and inspected him. His neck wound was strange. In the thin beam of the flashlight, I examined the skin at the base of his skull. There were deep bruises and internal bleeding where his spine had snapped, but I didn't think the damage had come from a blow.

I had seen one broken neck like his before. A truck had hit the back of a small car so hard the whiplash had snapped the driver's neck.

I went through his pockets and I found a cigarette lighter and a small pocketknife. There were no car keys. In his wallet were all his credit cards and over two hundred dollars in cash.

On a leather lace around his neck hung the Apache bead pouch, his good-luck charm that Jinks told me about. The beadwork mosaic was beautiful.

I stuffed the pouch back against his chest and the wallet back into his suit pocket. I was sure I would be arrested soon, and I didn't want to make Skinner's job easy.

In some nearby corrals, searching the ground with my

flashlight, I found about sixty feet of barbed wire which I dragged back to the well. I tied one end of it around Cass's chest under his arms.

Eventually there'd be a thorough autopsy, and I didn't want any more broken bones to cause confusion. I was already planning to call in the location of his body as soon as a rain came along and washed away my truck tracks to make an anonymous call possible. The cold water in the well would serve as a temporary morgue.

I tied a small rock to his right foot with a short piece of wire and got some leather gloves out of the back of my truck. Now that I was not so full of adrenaline, I realized how much Cass Boulding weighed as I lowered him over the side. Though I had my feet braced against the cement at the corner of the shaft, I was afraid the barbed wire would snag on my gloves and pull me headfirst down into the well after him.

Finally when he was in the water he became lighter and my muscles relaxed. I dropped the last of the wire in and shined my light down on the small ripples in the black water.

# 15

About two A.M. I arrived back in Phoenix. The ride there had been a nightmare. One after another the details of my life since sundown kept repeating themselves, this time as though under a magnifying glass.

I didn't want to go to Matt Gillette's house, so I called him from a pay phone and told him I had to talk to him within the hour about something vital. He agreed to meet me in the desert east of town. It was a place we had used before, when he was county attorney and his office and phones had been bugged.

On the way I made enough U-turns, tricks, stalls and clover-leaf rounds so that I was sure I hadn't been followed.

I arrived at the designated spot before Matt and I looked the place over with my flashlight. It was about two miles from the nearest paved road and not on any regular sheriff's route, so our only competition came from the lovers I surprised when I drove to the place where the dead-end road abutted the base of a cliff.

The lovers tried to wait me out, but within a few minutes their irritation at the silent dark presence of my truck behind them turned to fear. First his head appeared above the back of the seat, then hers, then he was dressing. His silhouette slipped behind the wheel and they roared away, their spinning wheels flinging rocks.

I felt sorry for interrupting them.

Matt showed up exactly when I expected him to, and we climbed to the top of a nearby hill. The moon shone down like an interrogation-room lamp, its light blue and rich. The desert was so quiet we could hear small animals all around us, so there was no chance of anyone sneaking up.

As we sat down I realized that I was going to try to get Matt to tell me I had done the right thing without telling him what I had done. I realized that was going to be impossible, but I began by making small talk.

"You hear from Kevin or Skyler or Bill?" They were the other three Coyotes.

"Nothing from Kevin. Postcard from Bill said he's holed up in a cabin in Alaska with every book he ever wanted to read, living on fish and poached venison. And Skyler's on that desert island in Mexico like he always planned. I'll bet he hasn't talked to another human being or worn a stitch of clothing for two months now."

"Matt. Matt," I said, slamming my palm down on the rock. "How in the hell are we ever going to beat them when we live like this."

"I don't know. But I do know we won't do anyone any

good if we become like them. If we use their tactics, we'll destroy ourselves."

In the bright moonlight I could make out Matt's features while he spoke. His tone was always reasonable, rarely angry, and usually tinged with humor. At first glance his face didn't seem strong; it was round—round nose and cheeks, and his light skin was always ruddy from the desert sun. But he was the kind of man people called at two in the morning for advice.

So I blurted it out: "Matt, Sheila Boulding hired me a few days ago to protect her ex-husband, Cass Boulding, you know, one of the Boulding Brothers. And he told me to get lost. Then tonight she had a birthday party for him and he didn't show. I think he was murdered."

Matt's eyes glittered in the moonlight.

"Call it a hunch," I said. "But assume I'm correct."

Matt watched my face to find out if I had misspoken when I used the word "hunch." During our work together "hunch" had become a code word between us meaning, roughly, *I know for sure but it is better if I don't tell you how I know*.

"I thought you weren't going to work this year," he said finally.

"Well, Jinks Boulding approached me. *She's* hard to turn down. Said I was the only one her mother felt she could trust."

"That's exactly what Cass Boulding told *me* when he came to me about six weeks ago," said Matt. His voice was infused with a tone I had heard him use once before when we traced a large real estate payoff through a

Mexican bank where funds were laundered and then transferred to various high-ranking Arizona officials, both Republican and Democrat.

"Told you what?" I asked.

"That *I* was the only one he trusted. He needed some tactical advice, and he said I was the only one he trusted. He'd never met me in person but he said I was the only one he trusted."

"Matt. What's going on? Two years ago Cass Boulding was part of the mob that ran you out of office. Now—"

"I'm sure Cass Boulding wanted my throat cut when we were trying to get him on that King Canyon land swindle. But he took our measure. And once he needed help—"

"What kind of tactical advice?" I asked.

"He said he had evidence of . . . his exact words were: 'very serious and dangerous fraud,' and he wanted to know how he could bring it out in the open. He said he knew for a fact the Arizona papers would not print his evidence nor investigate the situation."

"Not print his story? If anyone owned the papers, I thought he did."

"I told him that. Told him I thought the Phoenix *Sun* at least was in his own back pocket. He said: 'Not anymore.' He said there is a virtual 'news blackout in Arizona,' and that he personally knew why each and every high state official who had the power to do something wouldn't. I asked him to elaborate, and he said that 'all the closets were so full of skeletons the keys had been thrown away.' I asked him what that meant and he said, 'bribes.' I asked him how he knew for sure and he said: 'Because I paid them for years, and I wasn't the only one.' He said he couldn't go to the prosecutor's office now that I had been dumped, and he was angry at himself for helping dump me. I asked him to give me an idea of the fraud he had on his mind, and he said that powerless as I was I would only get myself killed with the information."

"So you have no idea what he had in mind?" I asked.

"None whatsoever."

"Any guesses?"

"Many. But I'm not going to mislead you with them. All I can say is, don't bother with anything petty. Cass Boulding was too much of a big crook to worry about a little oil in government machinery."

"You mean nothing like that scam to sell land over and over again to servicemen?"

"Well, there's millions of bucks involved there, but it wouldn't have bothered him. Not like he was bothered." Matt said.

"What kind of tactical advice did he want from you?"

"He wondered how to bring it all out in the open for the public to see. His only experience was in covering things up, and he had no idea how to bring them out. I asked him if it would make good national news, and he said yes. So I told him to send the material simultaneously to all the top newspapers in the country and to any national politicians he felt he trusted. He liked the idea, but he said he had about two thousand pages of technical data to back up what he was saying, and he thought that sending out that many large packages would arouse suspicion in the post office. So I suggested he microfilm the material and send a cover letter with each microfilm.

He wondered how big those packages would be, and I explained that two thousand pages would fit on ten small microfilm sheets."

I said, "He's got his own microfilm unit in his barn."

"There you go," said Matt. "Maybe he mailed the stuff last week, then disappeared for his own safety."

"He's safe," I said. "Safe enough for right now."

"Is that all you're going to tell me?"

"That's all you want to know. Right now, he disappeared, everyone will know that. No harm in your knowing it, too. It'll be in the papers tomorrow."

By any standard I was now already an accomplice after the fact in a first-degree murder, and there was no way I would implicate Matt Gillette by telling him too much.

"Is that all you're going to tell me?"

"Trust me, Matt. You know enough for now."

Heading home in the moonlight, I turned off the main road onto the private road leading to my house and stopped my truck. I opened my door and whistled and listened to the jingle of Bandit's dog tags as he loped from his waiting place beneath an ironwood tree and jumped across my lap to the seat beside me. He was shivering with delight and slapping his tail between the seat and dashboard. His white hair and black spots glistened in the blue moonlight. His tongue slopped across my face as I put my arm around him.

"Your daddy's got himself into some trouble, boy. But I didn't think it could have been helped. The whole Boulding thing was so complex . . . I had to blunder ahead and make mistakes to find out what is wrong somehow."

I shifted gears and Bandit lay down next to me and looked up out of his black mask. "You're going to start earning your keep again," I told him. "I'm going to need you to tell me what happens at home when I'm not here."

He began to calm down as he always did when I talked honestly to him.

I unclasped the collar around his neck and tossed it to the floor of the truck. The friendly jingle of his dog tags would be dangerous for him now as a watchdog. He needed to be able to move quietly through the desert at night.

I stroked the back of his neck and felt the tension there. Soon after the previous time I'd removed his collar he had caught someone sneaking up on my house on a dark night and he had been shot at. He must have connected the removal of his collar with that experience.

# 16

Next morning I awoke surprised to find I had not yet been arrested. I went outside and checked the back of my truck for blood or hair in the daylight. Not a trace. All the bleeding from his broken neck had been internal. I dressed, had breakfast and went to a public pool where I swam a mile to clear my head. Feeling somewhat refreshed and alive again, I bought a new pair of binoculars to replace the ones I had ruined.

At a corner newsstand I got the morning paper. Its top headlines were about the disappearance of Cass Boulding. One of the guards at the power plant swore he saw Cass Boulding leave at four in the afternoon; the other guard swore he never left at all.

In a related story, a scientist in the Atomic Energy Commission said Boulding's disappearance had no connection to the construction work Boulding Brothers was doing on the Phoenix Nuclear Facility.

I realized the worst thing I could do was make myself

scarce to the Boulding family. The best thing was to treat what happened last night as a nightmare. Then I could go to work. I certainly had enough of it to do.

Working outside the law and custom meant that my job was going to be incredibly difficult. If I still had been working for Matt Gillette, I would have had the use of police, of subpoenas, of the "so-help-you-god" oath and the perjury laws, of the press, of the courts and of public opinion. But now I had none of these. Worse, since I was an accessory after the crime, I no longer had full use of my own mind because I had to lie to avoid the memory of my experience.

Judging from the splash about Cass across the front page of the *Sun*, there would be many other men investigating to find out what happened to him. They would do it their way. And I would do it mine.

I drove the winding road to the Boulding ranch with dread, slowly. Even my engine seemed not to be running well. The tires felt low. High winds shook the truck and raised billowing clouds of dust. Then, on the straight part of the road about a mile from the ranch house, I saw fresh tracks which veered off the dirt road, over into the desert, and plowed to a stop in the soft dirt a hundred feet from the road. After that the tracks turned to the left and returned to the road and disappeared beneath other tracks.

It looked as if someone had lost the road on a straightaway. Had a drunk coming to the party not made all the sharp curves? The car had undoubtedly been going slow. Once off the road it had taken only a hundred feet to plow to a stop in the soft earth.

When I got to the ranch house, Claude Boulding came out the front door as I approached. He looked so much like Cass I was shocked.

"Morning. Your brother turned up yet?" I asked, my face and voice a mask of somber concern.

"I was going to ask you if you knew anything," he said. His face was worried.

"Does that young man know where Cass is?" came Gracious Boulding's voice through the open door.

"No, Mother, now stop worrying," he called back.

"Sounds like you've had your hands full with her," I said.

"Yeah, busier than cats burying crap," he said.

He closed the door and motioned for me to follow him to a corner of the front-yard cactus garden. He offered me a cigarette before telling me what he had on his mind.

"Sheila told me about you this morning," he said. "About hiring you. Her intuitions. I guess I didn't really notice you before. I bought Jinks's story. She certainly has enough boyfriends."

The wind blew in sudden gusts, then subsided, then blew again. Through the picture windows into the living-room I could see Gracious Boulding apparently talking to Jinks, while Sheila lay back in an easy chair and Joshua stood in front of the fireplace warming himself.

"Sheila told me about it because this whole business worries me," Claude continued. "She feels that Cass is in personal danger, but I have a feeling it is all directly connected to the antinuclear coalition. You know, they were mad when we beat them in the referendum."

The referendum had been part of the same election Matt Gillette lost.

"Suppose, as Jinks guessed, he is just off with a girl friend," I said, to see how he reacted.

"Let's hope so," said Claude and shuddered. I guessed he might be worried about his own life, too.

Joshua came outside to join us. He was wearing the same tattered clothes as the night before, and there were tiny yellow mesquite leaves in his uncombed hair and bushy beard. I guessed he had slept outside.

"Why haven't you investigated the coalition before now, before this crisis?" I asked Claude. "Do you feel threatened?"

"We did but our answers didn't come to much."

"Well, dammit, if you want me to do something, you'd better tell me all you know!" I said. "If I'd been told three days ago what you know, your brother might be standing here talking with us right now."

Joshua and Claude Boulding's eyes both fastened on me at the same instant, and I realized too late that my nightmare with Cass had leaked into my voice. My tone had said he was dead, and they'd both heard it. I realized the only way out of the questions in their eyes was forward.

I said, "I will assume the worst so that we have a basis for action. If he's in a hotel now getting laid, great. But if I don't assume the worst, I'm paralyzed; I can't work. It is also just plain sensible to assume the worst. That's the only way to keep it from happening."

Gradually their eyes relaxed as they thought about it.

I said, "Now tell me every damned thing you know or I'm going to take a vacation."

Claude kicked the toe of his boot in the dirt. "Well, it's not much. Immediately after the referendum several members of the coalition discussed the possibility of kidnapping or sabotage to show the public what they consider are the dangers of nuclear power."

"How did you hear about it?" I asked.

"An informant." Suddenly Claude's eyes shifted, corresponding to some internal shift in thought, and he said, "You don't like me, do you?"

"I hadn't spent any time on that question," I said. "And now isn't a good time to start."

"I know how you felt about Matt Gillette, but he had to go."

"I suppose he was bad for the economy," I said, "but enough of that for now. Do you take any precautions?"

"I have a bodyguard. He is in the back room right now. He was at the party with me last night and he is always at work. At the plant they think he's a nuclear engineer; other places they think he's a personal friend or an employee."

"Where is he now?"

"Watching us."

"Motion for him to show himself. I want to know what he looks like."

Claude gestured and Ralph Stark stepped around a corner of the house. He leaned against a wall and waited, glaring at me over the nose I had smashed all over his face.

"Nice company you keep," I said.

"I didn't hire him to be nice."

"He was fired from the police force for pistol-whipping an Indian kid."

"That was his recommendation," said Claude.

"Who'd Cass hire?" I asked.

"He thought a bodyguard was a damned nuisance. I kept after him about it until he gave Chato a pistol and told me that solved the problem. But it didn't. Neither of them took it seriously. Chato spends most of his time doing ranch work. He's just a Yaqui Indian cowboy and he's barely smart enough to flick his finger after he picks his nose."

"Where's Chato now?"

Joshua spoke for the first time: "Jinks's filly died about three this morning. By dawn Chato had buried her. Then he took a horse and rode west. He always does that when he feels bad. Two years ago he got drunk and wrecked Dad's truck and disappeared on a horse for a week."

At the same time Chato was disposing of Jinks's dead horse, I . . .

"I want to talk to him," I said.

"There's a couple thousand square miles out back," said Joshua. "You're welcome to try."

The bursts of wind were cutting through my clothing like cold water so I suggested we move inside. Sheila did not look up from the fireplace when we entered. Gracious Boulding was on the couch and Jinks was brushing her silvery hair with soothing strokes. It seemed to calm the old woman until she saw me, then she sat up straight and demanded, "Now you do something about my Cass.

That's your job. You paid him, didn't you, Sheila? You're working for us now, young man, and you're our only hope. When he was lost before, the Indian found him at dawn. This time he's been lost longer. Have you found that Indian yet?"

"He's dead, Grandma. Now hush?"

"Dead?" she shrieked.

"Chato's father has been dead for years, Grandma."

"You better find where that cave is. Have you found that cave?"

"That was a long time ago, Mrs. Boulding. I think this is a different situation," I said.

"Oh, you're just worthless. You slimy shithead."

"Grandma!"

"He is. He's worthless. Sheila, you never should have paid him. Now he won't work at all. He's just like a filthy Yaqui Indian. Once you pay them they go off and get drunk and you don't see them again till . . ."

"Hush, Grandma. Now hush," Jinks said.

But Jinks seemed most concerned about her mother. Sheila sat on the hearth looking into the fire, rocking gently back and forth and rubbing her neck. She didn't seem to be aware anyone else was in the room with her as she said, "That poor man has been tortured enough," in a voice full of remorse.

"Mom seems to be worse when you all are here," said Jinks.

Sheila Boulding turned from the fire to look at me and said, "Last night I dreamed I was drowning."

# Part Two

# 17

"There is no way to dramatize the 250,000 years of maintaining nuclear waste. I must go in the other direction.

"The institution of nuclear energy and waste will be considered, within one hundred years, similar to the institution of slavery. Equally as stupid. The actual costs were never calculated. If the 1977 New York City welfare costs were figured into the cost of slavery, the price of tobacco in 1808 would have been considerably higher.

"Even to have large amounts of radioactive waste lying around assumes a world which does not have: Latin American dictators, Joe Stalin, Charles Manson, suicidal American presidents, inquisitions, Hitler, General Idi Amin, South Africa, earthquakes, and insane mass movements such as surge through civilization with such regularity we must consider them normal.

"On a talk show recently an AEC member was asked what would happen if a bomb hit a nuclear storage dump. He answered that it would be no different than if one hit Washington, D.C. Not true. If Washington is hit with a bomb one year it will be rebuilt the next. If a nuclear storage dump is hit by a bomb it will be a wasteland for the next 250,000 years. The Phoenix bird will rise from its own ashes no more. The AEC scientist who gave this answer and misled the public will go on trial at Nuremberg 2001. His defense will be that he did not know any better, that his government told him what to say. No matter. His sentence will be life at hard labor, studying history."

Jinks wore earphones and was listening to her father's voice. She wrote out passages she considered significant. Next to her on the table were hundreds of hours of Cass's unprocessed diary. Judging by the look of determination on her face, Jinks would not rest until she had heard it all.

There was no doubt she and Joshua had been working all night. Her apartment had been torn apart and rearranged for action. The kitchen table, a coffee table and a card table were placed along the walls and were covered with small cardboard boxes. At the base of every box were note cards detailing the contents. Stuck into the walls with tacks were penciled notes.

Through a sliding glass door at the back of the apartment I saw a landscaped patio. In the middle of it stood an ancient mesquite tree. Beneath the tree, among the mulch of the tiny yellow leaves, lay a blue sleeping bag where Joshua evidently had taken whatever rest he'd had the night before.

While I had been disposing of Cass Boulding, his son and daughter had moved into action to try to find him alive. Jinks watched my face as I read the quotes she had written, and the passionate intensity of her eyes brought first heat and then a terrible stinging into my own eyes as I remembered Cass sinking slowly into the well.

I was saved from having to try to talk to her then by her doorbell.

She opened the door and a man burst in. He rushed into the living room, gave Joshua and me a look that was not friendly, surveyed the working area and said:

"I read it in the morning paper and caught the first flight. What happened?" His voice was not questioning, it was angry. "Who are these men? Do you have any scotch?"

"You should have called," said Jinks.

"I wanted to be with you," he said.

"You should have called."

"Where's the scotch?" He moved into the kitchen area and began opening cupboards. "Who are those men?" he asked over his shoulder.

"Not now, Larry. I can't explain to you now."

He found the scotch, ice and a glass, and while he was pouring asked again, "What happened?"

"You should have called first."

"Who are these men, dammit? Tell me what happened."

"I can't talk now. I'm too busy with all this."

Larry swallowed a mouthful of scotch.

His skin had the consistency of dough, though it was

covered with a veneer of tan. He was dressed expensively.

"I want to know one thing," he said, pointing at Jinks.

"Put your finger in your pocket or I'll cut it off," snapped Joshua.

"Who are these guys?" Larry asked, lowering his hand.

"What do you want, Larry?"

He didn't point at her this time. "Are you going to be ready for the Denver concert?"

"There's no way I can know, so I can't tell you."

"You can't tell me!" His voice was filled with astonished mockery.

"When I know more about Dad, I'll call you. Now go back to Los Angeles."

"Go back to Los Angeles? Go back to Los Angeles!" His voice became shrill.

"Please, Larry."

"Who are these guys? Are they from Columbia?"

Jinks broke. "He's my brother, goddam you," she screamed and picked up the glass he had just put down and threw it at his head from point-blank range and missed. "He's my goddam brother, you . . ." Words failed her, but her feet and flying hands did not. She pummeled, scratched and kicked him out the front door, slammed it and leaned against it, sobbing.

Five minutes later the phone rang. Calmed by now, she answered it, listened, then hung up without saying a word. She made herself a cup of coffee and went back to listening to her father's diary and taking notes.

All day long we listened to the diary and went through

Cass's personal papers. Joshua still had not brushed the tiny yellow leaves from his hair and beard, and he drank many cups of mountainman coffee which he made by filling a cup half full of coffee grounds and then adding hot water. His eyes blazed and the veins in his forehead and neck stood out, but he worked quietly and methodically, listening to the chanting voice of his father for patterns. And he sweated. The green shirt he was wearing turned a darker color from the perspiration.

Early in the afternoon he took a shower, and when he emerged from the bathroom his hair was pasted back, revealing more of his broad forehead than I had seen before. Creeping out of his hairline was a scar. I asked him how he got it.

"Tell you later. Long story. We've got too much work here for now."

Not long after that we ran out of coffee and he left to get more.

When he had driven away I asked Jinks how he got the scar.

"In Hong Kong he got in a bar fight with several Australians. He didn't have any weapons so he grabbed one of them by his ears and used his own head like a battering ram on the other man's head."

I laughed. I needed to laugh to relax and the image of Joshua butting heads with an Australian was all I had to laugh at.

"I suppose I'd find it funny, too," said Jinks, "but the man died. Joshua ran away from the bar and got away with it, but he was nearly crazy with the memory of it when he got back to Phoenix. He wouldn't talk to a shrink about it, so he used me instead. I thought I was going to go crazy from listening to him the first few months after he got back."

We took a break from the tapes when the afternoon news came on. Both major television networks we watched reported Cass's disappearance. Both said there was as yet no evidence of foul play. A Phoenix television station did not even mention Cass's disappearance, but spent three minutes' camera time poking around the city dump near the spot where a human hand and foot had been found. The late owner of the items had been a midwestern Teamsters official. Phoenix coverage of corruption in other places was excellent.

It was dark when I suggested we all get some rest. Jinks, who had been listening to tapes and taking notes all day long, looked very weary. She came over to the table at which I had been working and handed me a sheet of notes.

Gunk is so hot it will boil for the next 250,000 years. It is so caustic it destroys its own stainless steel containers. No metal had yet been developed which gunk will not disintegrate within twenty years. A significant spill will destroy all mammal life in areas the size of Arizona for seven million five hundred thousand human generations.

When radioactive material reaches a watershed area, it will be dispersed into the ocean and spread.

Plutonium is the stuff of which bombs are made. The General Accounting Office in Washington reports 11,000 pounds of weapons grade material, enriched uranium and plutonium, is unaccounted for. Is there a black market? There is enough material floating around to make 363 bombs all larger than the one dropped on Hiroshima.

"So far as we know, everybody in the world who has tried to make a nuclear explosion since 1945 has succeeded on the first try."

—TED TAYLOR, conceptual designer of nuclear bombs at Los Alamos scientific laboratory who designed Davy Crockett and Hamlet.

While I read, Jinks put her arms around Joshua and hugged him fiercely. When I had finished and looked up, she saw the look on my face, came to me and hugged me, too. She sat down on the floor next to me and took the open palm of my hand and rubbed her face in it. She kissed my fingers. When she started to relax I swung around behind her and rubbed the back of her neck. She sobbed. Joshua knelt down on the floor beside her and hugged her while I rubbed the tension from her shoulders.

# 18

"When the stakes were low and the desert was still fresh
and virgin, I did not mind the bribes. I didn't have to pay
much attention to them anyway, since Claude was the
master at passing out cash without offense or detection.
One hundred dollar bills, crisp. Seven of them to the real
estate commissioner, four to each of three highway
commissioners. Here's a few for the planning and zoning
committee and here's . . . now, everybody's happy for the
month, get on with business as usual. How else could it
have been done? It wasn't hurting anyone. It was oil for
the machinery of free government. But what I didn't
realize was that we good old Arizona boys were getting
each other into the habit of taking money for favors, and
now that the sun is for sale, the big bucks are rolling in.
And they have so much cash now that Arizona is being
Californicated, as Joshua says, and New Jerseyed and
New Yorked and Michigoosed. And they have no respect for the institutions that allowed them to rise. They

*kill reporters, witnesses, competition and maybe Presidents. And Claude wants to cooperate with them, because they have the capital.*

*"And into this stew of corruption the fools want to bring nuclear power. And nuclear waste."*

The following morning Jinks and I were again listening to Cass Boulding's diary when the phone rang.

Jinks answered and listened for a while before she said, "I don't want you here right now, Larry." Then she listened again for a while before she slammed the phone.

She hadn't removed her hand from the phone when it rang again. She picked it up, already screaming, "Don't tell me you love me, you bastard. You don't love me. You use me. And now I'm useless to you. So fuck off!"

She paused, listened, and her rage dissolved. She dropped the phone and walked out of the room. I picked up the phone where she had dropped it and said hello.

"What's going on?" asked Joshua.

"She thought you were Larry."

"I wish I were Marie Antoinette. God, have I got a headache. All that listening to Dad's diary is too painful. I think I'll stay in bed all day."

A couple of hours later Jinks gave me some insight into why Joshua was having such a headache. I was listening to the diary when I heard Cass Boulding say: *"Loving Joshua taught me to love. Any fool can love his own son, but to love a son issuing from Sheila's hate simply because that child is helpless and needs loving, that is a learning chore. But one well worth it. Joshua taught me more than any natural son could have. . . ."*

I tapped Jinks on the shoulder. She took off her earphones, and I played the passage again.

After it was over she said, "I was hoping there wouldn't be any references to that in the parts you listened to. It's not relevant to Dad's disappearance."

"I can't know that until I've heard it."

"What the hell. I'm embarrassed, but you're becoming part of the family anyway. You may as well know our secrets, too. Joshua isn't Dad's son."

"I'm not quite sure why that's so terrible. Was Sheila married before?"

"Mother and Dad were married three years before Joshua was born. Then me, the following year."

"Sounds like he forgave her quickly."

"He didn't know. Not until much later."

"How do you know all this?"

"Conversations with Mother and Gracious. Mother has never said it directly, but when she is especially angry, she alludes to it. You'd have to have been there to know for sure, but it's true."

"Angry?"

"She got mad at him for something and hurt him the only way she knew how. That was after the war and motherhood was the rage then, so motherhood was the weapon. I'm lucky. I can fight with my hands, if necessary, and I can use my songs. Mother came out of a different world, and she only knew how to use what she used."

"You're sure about this? He certainly looks like a Boulding."

"Genetics or emulation, who knows which forms the face?"

"I'm still not clear about how you knew."

"I listened to what Mother felt when she spoke— rather than to what she said."

"Could Joshua have done this?"

"I don't think so. Men don't know how to listen to what a woman feels when she talks. It's a private language. Like men in a locker room. But he might have heard. He's pretty sensitive, perceptive."

"Well, that answers the question your mother side-stepped that first day I met her."

"What was that?"

"Why Cass would be so angry at her as to be throwing punches in his sleep."

Had Cass Boulding kept a diary in the conventional way, I could have read through thousands of pages in an afternoon, skimming over the surface like a fishing bird, dropping into it when I spotted something relevant. But listening to the tapes was listening to his mind unwind. It went on and on.

Side by side and inextricably linked were public and private situations. One minute he would be talking about nuclear energy, the next about his feelings for his family.

"We are hearing the private life of nuclear energy," Jinks said during one of our coffee breaks.

Sometimes Cass was so depressed he could barely speak. Sometimes, when a situation came clear to him, he was elated. He spoke of hating the people he loved most, or of loving the people he hated most. Sometimes he laughed at puns he made, sometimes he laughed bitterly at his own mistakes. Once in the middle of talking about Sheila he fell silent for several minutes and forgot to turn off the recorder. Just before he fell silent he had been furious at himself for his inability to: *". . . hear my own wife clearly, to hear what it is she says to me rather than what I am saying to myself with her voice in my mind at the moment she is talking to me."*

I became convinced that the envelopes to newspapers in the missing briefcase contained something connected to the Phoenix Nuclear Power Facility.

*"Nuclear scientists are no more to be trusted with the future of life on our planet than the International Teamsters' Union or the Mafia. In matters historical, political and humanistic, they are no more wise or moral than those organizations.*

*"A nuclear-powered society will place into the hands of a few the largest concentration of power over the greatest number of people in the history of the world.*

*"Atomic energy will cause the death of democracy. The dangers of the misuse of atomic materials are so severe, a police state will form to protect society from its own creation. The torture of thousands of people will literally become justifiable to protect millions from destruction. The sadists will gather together in this police state, as they did under Stalin, but they will never disband, because the basis for their gathering, the nuclear waste materials, will not go away.*

*"I have been more guilty than most of the destruction*

112

of nature, the *wilderness which has always nourished man's higher instincts. If it were not for Joshua and the example of his life I probably never would have seen my way out of the fortress I built around myself. My materials: possessions—wife, incessant labor, money, bulldozers, prestige and power.*

*"Joshua taught me to read. When I was down he handed me Dostoevski, and I began to understand the incredible complexity of my feelings, the atomic structure of my soul. When I could stand again he gave me Erich Fromm, who helped me put it all together into a moral framework, to see the significance of my most obscure impulses in the mirror of world events."*

Not long after lunch, in a tape made three weeks ago (all the tapes from two weeks ago to the present were missing) I found some immediate evidence.

*"No matter what I do, Skinner and friends will swallow the evidence like a shark. The Phoenix Sun is not even publishing the series generated by the murder of the grand jury witness. Probably no place outside the Soviet Union is the news so carefully controlled as in Phoenix. The big money literally has the power to create its own version of reality.... They will kill me and destroy my work."*

Two hours' listening time later, I heard something that seemed to connect to Cass's earlier thoughts.

*"The big news. News. News. News. News. News. Kidnapping. Kidnapping, yeah. Kidnapping is the most interesting subject imaginable to a nation of people*

*whose souls have been kidnapped by cars and television
and electric masturbators. Kidnapping is my solution. I
must be kidnapped, kidnap myself. That is the only way
to stay alive and the only way to leap over the money-
green wall of news suppression in Phoenix."*

Even though I was exhausted by then, I went on
listening, hoping for more entries that would link to the
references to Les Skinner and to Cass kidnapping himself. But there was only more philosophical thought and
references to family. By then I began to realize that what
I feared most had happened. Cass had some system for
disposing of the most dangerous tapes. I could not have
figured this out earlier because he made his diary entries
at random. There was no way for me to tell the differ-
ence between a day in which he made no entries from
one in which he destroyed the entries he made. Before
the afternoon was over I had learned most of the general
details to be learned by listening to this oral diary. To get
at the particulars, I needed the contents of the briefcase
that had been slammed on my hand.

# 19

*"There are three evils which modern science has in no way alleviated: human destructiveness, the disposal of nuclear waste and death. . . . The next Hitler will have better tools to use while acting out his destructiveness."*

The sun had just set when Joshua came in. He had said he was going to stay in bed to get over "the memories," but he didn't look rested. His clear blue eyes seemed tired and set a little farther back in his head, and there was a rosy bloom on his nose and cheeks.

"Feel better?" I asked.

"Yeah. Stayed in bed and buried my head in a pillow."

He wasn't a good liar. Good liars look you straight in the eye and form their faces in a mask of sincerity, and they don't make mistakes. Joshua answered to my right shoulder, and he forgot that the skin on his face registered the fact that he had been out in the sun that day.

Sheila had predicted Cass Boulding's disappearance,

Chato couldn't be found, and now Joshua was lying to me.

I decided to lean on him for a while, to trap him into some more lies which he would have to explain when I confronted him.

"I was thinking of your mother's prediction. She seems to have called your father's disappearance pretty accurately."

"I was thinking about that, too," he said, and the telephone rang. He fell silent and we watched while Jinks answered it.

She listened a while before she said, "It doesn't matter what day it is. I won't consider giving that concert tomorrow in Denver."

She listened again and said, "Don't lay that on me, Larry. I have not been the least bit vague about all this. You've been stringing them along, haven't you? I told you to call off the concert and you told them I'd make it. Isn't that right? And you've been popping the reds again, haven't you. I won't talk to you anymore if you call me strung out again. Words don't mean anything to you when you're like this."

She spoke calmly and grimly. Joshua watched the coffee swirl sluggishly around the bottom of his coffee cup, and I noticed the redness on the backs of his hands.

"Can't you hear me, Larry? The contract doesn't mean anything if I'm ill.... Damn you, most sickness is not bacterial.... Look, I'm not going to argue with you anymore. Cancel the concert! Cancel all engagements until I call you!"

"As I was saying," said Joshua when she sat down

116

again, flushed and furious, then rose and began clearing our dinner dishes as though she wanted to break them.

"Let me help," I said.

"Get out of my way."

"As I was saying," said Joshua. "I've come to the conclusion that there are three powers Mother could possess which would give her deeper intuitions than the rest of us. The first is keen observation. For years she's been able to watch, let's say, a President on television and know when he is lying. The rest of us have to wait for years for the lies behind the mask to emerge, but she picks up the tiniest clues, actually seems to perceive them instead of what the rest of us perceive.

"I also suspect she has the ability to actually see what people are dreaming and to hear what they are hearing in their own head. I'm positive about this because I've seen her do it."

"But the one that bothers me most is that I'm afraid discarnate spirits sometimes speak through her."

Joshua seemed quite sincere, and I was astonished that he was actually throwing me such a line of crap to distract me from his red nose.

"It's all a bit primitive for me," I said.

"So it's come to that, then," said Joshua. "You too confuse gadgets with wisdom. Maybe you'd say Shakespeare is a primitive? Or Sophocles is a primitive? You too think that the simple accumulation of technical data amounts to wisdom. Compare for me, if you would, the intelligence of the man who wrote *Macbeth* with the man who hit the golf ball on the moon."

"I would, Joshua, but it would get me off the subject.

The subject is: Why are you lying? Where has Chato gone? How did your mother actually predict—"

"Lying?"

"You spent the day in bed getting over your headache and the memories?"

"Yes."

"Then there must not be a roof on your house, because your face shows sun and wind burn. I don't know why you're lying, Joshua, but it doesn't look good to me. And I'm sure it will look worse at the Sheriff's Office. I'm going to talk to you as your friend for a little while longer, but unless you tell me what you did today, I'm going to make a phone call. After that it's not going to be like talking to your friend and your sister."

"Don't get in my way, Falconer," said Joshua, and his eyes flashed with menace. He spoke quietly but a note in his voice shifted my weight from my seat to my toes. He glared at me, letting me know I had gone too far by uncovering his lie, and we were both rising from our chairs before I realized he would welcome a fight as a relief from uncertainty. I bowed my head slightly, feigning submission, and sat back down. My retreat seemed to confuse him, and he too sat back down, blinking heavily.

Jinks came over and took his chin in her hand. Slowly she turned his face up and examined his skin. Her interrogation was totally silent. Whereas my threats had hardened him, her quiet loving questions unleashed the truth.

"I was out looking for Dad," he said to Jinks. "You remember that series of springs in among the red cliffs on the west end of the old ranch? Well, I thought he might be there. It had always been a special, sacred place for me, and Dad once told me he felt the same way about it. I wanted to tell you but when Dad told me he was going to disappear, he swore me to secrecy. He said that only Chato and I knew, and that to tell anyone else might get him killed. Dad killed."

"He told you he was going to disappear?" I asked.

"The night before his party. He said that twenty-four hours after his party he was going to have to disappear for several months and that he would need me to be the family spokesman for him. He told me I was to share the version of what happened to him that everyone else had, but that he would have to disappear, to seem to be kidnapped."

"To kidnap himself?"

"Yes, he said he would have to kidnap—yes, he used those words. We were at his house, the new one, and he was in the process of telling me his plans when he was interrupted by a phone call. After he hung up he was in too much of a hurry to tell me more. He said he wanted to meet me after his party was over and explain the rest to me. And he told me twice more that if I softened and told Mother or Jinks or Gracious what he had told me about kidnapping himself, it might get him killed. He took me by the shoulders when he told me and I could see he meant it. I asked him why, and he said because their grief and worry for him should be absolutely real, or else it could cost him his life. He said he would explain the rest to me right after the party. He was in a terrible hurry and he was frustrated because nothing was coming out in the right order. He said there would be intense news coverage, and he couldn't take a chance on letting anyone else in on it. He said he let me in on it only because he would need me to do some things."

"Like what?"

"He was in too much of a hurry to say."

"Somewhere in there I told him I was afraid the worry would kill Grandma. The thought of it seemed to upset him, but he soon recovered and said that would be better than the alternative, which might be the killing of Jinks's and my unborn children."

"Kidnap himself?" I asked. "He said those words?"

"Yes. How did you know them?" Joshua asked me.

"Heard them on one of his tapes. Probably when the idea first came to him."

"Kidnap himself," Jinks said, shook her head and mused.

"He said he would explain to me right after the party and then his plan would go into action the next day."

"The plan?"

"I've told you all I know. Oh, yeah, now I remember. When I told him I thought this was needlessly cruel for the family, he answered that Claude and Sheila must not know about it, that Gracious couldn't guard a secret with a shotgun and that Jinks was such a public figure it might slip out."

"Then he's all right," said Jinks. Her voice was brimming with emotion.

"Except he disappeared a day before he said he would," said Joshua. "Without telling me why."

"He's all right," said Jinks, not listening to him or bothering to catch a look at my face. "And no one will catch the slightest hint of it from anything I do or say. And you, Daniel, you will—"

"I can keep a secret."

"The canceled concert is just what he wants," she said. "They will make a big thing of it on the news and that is just what he wants. His putting us through all this. . . . He must have a good reason. He's alive." She began to weep with relief.

Her fingers trailed across my shoulders as she walked out of the room and down the hallway and into her bedroom. Then she began to sing. She sang as though giving every ounce of herself to the thousands who would be turning in their tickets in Denver, and she sang all her best poetry to an empty room with her voice cracking under the pressure of her intense, vain hopes.

# 20

"Even if doing what I am doing costs me my life, I must continue.

"Today I explained to Chato the dangers he incurs by working with me. 'No le hace,' he said. It is fascinating to me that this man who can't even read can still understand what must be done. . . . Maybe it isn't so strange that a human being doesn't want to destroy his grandchildren. . . . Claude was drunk and nasty the other night. He said he doesn't care whether his great-grandchildren die or have three heads, he wants his electricity now. . . . Cancer is on the rise near the Colorado nuclear plant.

"I will inform Joshua at the last minute—just before I disappear. There is so much work to do now, I need him badly; but he is too unstable, I'm afraid. I can never figure out how much of his craziness is real and how much is an act."

"Daniel," she said, "Daniel, I killed him." Jinks's fingers groped across my chest in search of my face. After she'd gone into her room, I'd fallen asleep on the couch.

"I killed him." Her voice pleaded with me. I had been in the middle of a dream but now it was gone.

"Who?"

"Dad."

"How?"

"I squeezed him to death. I was crying and hugging him and begging, like a little girl, love me, love me, because I never really felt he loved me. It was never quite me he loved. Always someone else, slightly, my twin, he was loving."

"And you killed him?"

"I broke his neck. And I seemed to know what I was doing while doing it. I kept saying, '*I love you to death, I love you to death.*'"

She put her arms around me. My thoughts were not yet waking thoughts.

"When did this happen?" I whispered, since her ear was touching my lips.

"Right after I stopped singing, I was so tired then, like a child after a good cry, and I fell asleep. All these fears for Dad's safety dredged up terrible dreams. In the one just before I hugged him to death, I was standing on the edge of a cliff when the edge broke. I grabbed the new edge and that boulder broke loose, and so on, the next and the next."

Hearing her at last I asked, "Do you have any idea why?"

"He didn't love me. When he told me he thought I

shouldn't sing because of the bad company I would keep, he wasn't loving me."

"How so?"

"He was loving his dream of me, not me. When I was fourteen I stayed out all night and when I came in he said he was disappointed in me. He became all dreamy and said that any man I would want to marry would want a virgin for a wife, and I saw in the glaze in his eyes that he was talking to some mythical daughter. For God's sake, there I was, already not a virgin, and there he was ripping away my young-girl dreams of a husband. If he had loved me he would have also loved my needs."

"And for that you killed him?"

"Only in the dream, Daniel. But I hurt him a lot in reality. I screwed a lot of guys I didn't love just to shove the knife into that selfish dream he had of his daughter, Jinks Boulding. If he ever could have said, some way, '*I love you as you are,*' I could have stopped screwing men I didn't love and quit hurting myself. As it was, I probably caused him more anxiety than seven subdivisions."

"All because it wasn't quite you he loved?"

"He loved my surface. My surface responded with love, but my insides responded with hatred for his not understanding me. I didn't understand it at the time; I just thought that was the way I was, liking to screw lots of different men, being unable to love any one. I didn't understand how much I enjoyed watching him squirm. Then I got into the same situation with Larry."

"Your manager, Larry? I don't understand him with you. Ten o'clock in the morning and he barges into your apartment and wants a scotch. I don't understand him at all. He's a lightweight. You're not."

"He wasn't like that when I met him. If he's a lightweight now it's because I turned him every way but loose. His main problem was that he couldn't walk away from me when I . . . look, I had more games than a toy store. . . . Poor Larry. Did he really seem like a lightweight?"

"He needed half dollars in his pockets to keep from blowing away."

"Larry had an ideal; he wanted to love me like I am. He told me that when we started. So I told him everything. Dad wouldn't listen to my needs, but Larry listened to them all. I told him about every man I had screwed before him, and I told him about every man I screwed while he and I were together. He had this ideal of loving me like I was, not trying to change me, and he kept saying, 'I want to know it all, I want to love you as you are.' I told him everything, every position. There you go."

*There you go,* she had said, *There you go.* Whenever I saw suddenly into the heart of a situation, Matt Gillette had said, *There you go.* She knew Matt.

"What aren't you telling me?"

"About what?"

"I'll leave the question open."

"Daniel, you're mad."

"I'm suddenly feeling like a pawn, and I don't know whose game or the rules."

"Your shoulders tensed up like you're ready for a fight."

In the dark we lay face to face on the couch, our arms around each other. She started to reach to turn on a lamp, but I restrained her. I didn't want to see her right then. I wanted to listen to her in the dark. Her voice was so rich with meaning; she couldn't lie to me in the dark.

"I'm listening."

"To what? What do you want me to say?"

"Don't say what I want you to say; say what you feel. Say what I want you to say and you'll start hating me, too. Say what you feel."

"Ooh wee," she said. "Another part of that dream just came back. I can't remember it now ... yes, Mother was in it. She was me. Sometimes it wasn't me hugging Dad to death, it was her. Sometimes it was her and sometimes me."

"I don't quite see the connection."

"Just a feeling I have right now. That she did the same thing with Dad as I did with Larry. That her doing it with Dad grew out of both her feelings for her father and for Dad, that her mother before her ... oh, I have so many memories now. So many voices from when I was a kid. I see the ranch house on a clear spring morning and I'm only half the height of a horse and I'm feeling like I know what I'm going to do when I'm old enough to do it. Like I knew what Mother did and I was going to do the same thing when I was old enough. God, I don't want to be like her."

"What did she do?"

"I don't know. The business with Joshua. Eichh."

"How did you know you were going to do it if you didn't know what it was?"

"I just knew, that's all. I knew what she must have done only in some intuitive way, and I didn't know what I was going to do until I did it. Poor Larry. He walked into so many traps."

"*There you go,*" I said. I did something to my voice to make it sound like Matt Gillette's.

Her shoulders tensed again. "Did Matt tell you . . ."

"No. You did."

"I did?"

"What about you and Matt?"

"Mother didn't get your name out of the newspaper. She told me about her fears for Dad and when I told Matt about it, he suggested I call you. He said the way your mind worked, if anyone could do something to protect Dad, you could. He said of all the investigators he knew, you could penetrate all this the quickest."

"I wish I was quicker. Maybe Matt overestimated me."

"He said you wouldn't get caught up in the trivia."

"I'm trying. Now what about you and Matt?"

"What about? Oh—well, we were lovers. He helped me learn about my feelings. He was the first man who ever understood me and helped me understand myself."

"More."

"It's hard to talk when you're so tense."

"Get me out of the dark and I'll probably relax."

"I'd just left Larry—for the last time—and come back to Phoenix to lick my wounds. I was still bound to Larry as my manager by contracts, but I was determined the other thing was over. And I met Matthew one day. He knew me from my albums, and I knew him because Dad and Uncle Claude hated him so much from his county attorney days. I guess they had their tails in a lot of cracks, and they were always afraid he would slam the doors."

"We tried, but they had too much money."

"So Matt was a natural for me. I didn't realize it at the time, of course, I simply thought he was very sexy, which he is, and bright and sensitive, which he is. One night we were making love and in the middle of it he stopped. He got up, dressed in silence, and said he would be back soon and walked out of his house. He was gone for about an hour, and I thought I was going nuts. When he came back in he sat down on the bed next to me and said, 'Do you know what a tool is? It's something you use to get a job done, like a knife. When we were making love it suddenly came to me that I was your tool. Now whom are you stabbing with me?' My jaw began to quiver and I began shaking and crying and denying what he had said. Then I broke down and cried for several hours. After that we talked for days, and I began to realize and understand the things I told you ending with my dream of killing Dad."

"Why aren't you with Matt now? Why are you lying here with your arms around me?"

"He says I'm not ready for him as a lover, and I think he's right. I keep hearing a little voice, the one that usually gives me my songs, saying, 'Don't inflict yourself on Matt. He doesn't deserve you.'"

"But I do."

"No, you don't either."

"Who are you stabbing with me?"

She began to weep, and though I didn't know if it was the right thing to do, I hugged her gently.

"Oh, I'm so lonely," she said. "Poor Larry. Poor Dad. Poor all of us."

# 21

"There will be a trial at Nuremberg in the year 2001. My grandchildren will raid the retirement communities, arresting the politicians, engineers and bureaucrats of my generation. The charge: creation of millions of tons of nuclear waste. They will ask why we did it; we will answer we had no choice. We will be charged guilty of self-deception. The penalty: death."

"Caring means caring not only for our fellow beings on this earth but also for our descendants. Indeed, nothing is more telling about our selfishness than that we go on plundering the raw materials of the earth, poisoning the earth, and preparing nuclear war. We hesitate not at all at leaving our own descendants this plundered earth as their heritage."

Erich Fromm,
*To Have or to Be*

"Who is this?"

"Falconer."

"What are you doing in Jinks's apartment?"

"Looking over some things and trying to figure out what happened to your son."

"I'm the only one home now. Chato rode up a little while ago and unsaddled his horse, and before he could drive away I invited him into the house. He's in the kitchen now. I gave him a bottle of wine."

"Who else have you told?" I motioned to Jinks who went into the bedroom and picked up the other extension and listened.

"I wanted to keep him here for you. He's never liked me and the only way I could get him to stay was to give him some—"

"Grandma," said Jinks. "Are you all right?"

"Chato came back. He's in the kitchen now. I gave him a bottle of wine."

"Let me talk to him," said Jinks.

"No. Hush. Hurry. He'll leave."

"Grandma, let me talk to him. If I tell him to wait there to talk to me, he'll—"

A loud cracking interrupted.

"Jinks?"

"She must have dropped the phone," said Jinks.

Immediately I had several different images of why Gracious dropped the phone, most of them involving violence to her. There was nothing to do but wait.

Gracious's voice again, "Oh, dear. He snuck away. That wino stole the entire bottle and drove away! He drove away, Jinks! I knew I shouldn't have left him alone."

"Who else have you told?"

"Goddam son-of-a-bitch heathen Mexican bastard Indian asshole wino," said Gracious Boulding.

I hung up and shouted at Jinks, "Ask her again. She can't hear the sound of my voice."

Jinks asked, "Who else have you told, Grandma?"

But all Gracious did was cuss. And hang up.

The wind was strong and dust came in to cover Phoenix. We drove down out of the foothills into the brown surface as though into a sea of mud.

In the Mexican *barrio* there were children in the streets. They played soccer and threw baseballs, oblivious of the cars around them, seemingly too full of vitality to ever be subdued by schools and soul-destroying jobs and time.

The house where Chato lived had not yet been reached by urban renewal. Built in the old Spanish style around the turn of the century, its walls were two feet thick and its ceilings fifteen feet high. Chato had lived there, Jinks said, since she was a child, keeping his horse and a few chickens in the backyard until zoning forbade it, then selling the horse and moving the chickens indoors with the family into a special coop off the kitchen. It was the kind of dwelling that intrigued tourists who blundered past it, but it was built more sturdily than any dwellings in the past fifty years. But I knew that the lawyers would soon discover it, as they had discovered nearby neighborhoods, and they would drive out the families like Chato's with higher taxes and rents, and the building would be "restored," would become "historic," a lawyer's office.

Chato's wife, Melba, embraced Jinks and took us through the dark echoing rooms to a room at the back where Chato lay face up in a sagging bed, the pit of his elbow covering his eyes. When Melba shook him he groaned and pushed her away and rolled toward the wall.

Then he heard Jinks's voice and struggled to rise and become conscious, but the sunlight stung his squinting eyes, and he fell back, groaning angrily. Melba went into the kitchen, while chickens clucked in the background, as Jinks talked to him and he tried to listen. Soon Melba returned with a pan of ice water and a washcloth. She worked on him with firm strokes, rubbing his face and chest with the icy cloth. After she had him sitting up on the side of the bed holding his face in his hands, she left and returned with scalding black coffee.

"Chato," I said, when he could talk at last, "we need to know something. When Cass was working at his new ranch in his office, he was microfilming important papers. We need to know if you helped him."

He looked at me and shrugged as though he didn't speak English.

"Chato, please talk to us," said Jinks.

"*Lo siento mucho que pasó con su caballo,*" he said to Jinks. He was sorry about the death of her horse.

"That wasn't your fault, Chato. You did all you could possibly do."

By then children were crowding in at the door to the

room. Chato made a threatening motion toward them and they dispersed like quail. Melba followed them out of the room and closed the door.

*"Lo siento mucho,"* he said. *"Era muy bella y ahora es muerta."* The filly was very beautiful and now she is dead. If men were judged by their capacity to feel kindness toward animals, Chato would be king.

Jinks said, "Chato, listen to me. We need you to tell us something about Dad. We think something bad has happened to him."

A startled look spread the hungover wrinkles around his eyes, and I could see he was just beginning to realize we had not come to talk about the dead filly.

"Did you help Cass when he was microfilming papers in his new barn?" I asked.

*"Sí, señor."* Suddenly I felt that he might listen to English in his own house even if he was too proud to speak it there.

"Did you read any of the papers you were microfilming?" I asked.

*"No, señor, no puedo leer Inglés. No puedo. Solo meté los papeles en la máquina y los saqué cuando terminaron."* He did not read English. He only put the papers into the machine and took them out when the machine was through with them.

He squinted at us and rubbed his face. He seemed very confused. He had been thinking of the death of the filly and his betrayal of Jinks's trust, and now suddenly here we were with an urgent need to know the details of something he didn't understand when he did it. I was sure that Cass must have told him never to talk about the work they had done together.

"Dad has disappeared." said Jinks.

"*Cassandro? Donde?*"

"Disappeared," she said. "We don't know where. You must tell us what you know so we can find him."

He searched our eyes for answers, and the wine still ran its blurring fingers over his face.

Then he stood up and marched to me until our chests were nearly touching. He brought his forearm up to my chest and put a hand on my shoulder, saying, "You're a good man," then to Jinks, "This man, he's good. When I talk to him I feel raised up. I am stronger. Other men with their eyes, they make you feel low. I already feel so low sometimes I don't know why men want me to feel lower. Sometimes I'm already so low I'm in a hole. But this man, he's good. He's the only one I ever seen with you that's good, Jinks. All the others, they're all bad. Everybody you know is bad except Joshua. You and him made Cassandro better. Cassandro, he used to be a terrible man, but he's a good man now."

"Please, Chato, tell us what you did in the barn so we can find Dad," said Jinks.

Chato stepped away from me, summoning his will to communicate, trying to push his drunkenness away. Then, since he felt he didn't have the right words to describe what he had done for Cass, he began to mime. He told us we were behind the grain bags full of sand and where each machine was, and where the large tables were, and where the desk was. He went over and over it;

with each motion he performed, I asked him what he had done.

He picked up a large pile of papers nearly a foot thick and put them on one table. I asked him questions about these papers and found out there were probably a thousand pages of material, some typed, some diagrammed, some handwritten.

One by one he put them onto the scanner of the microfilm machine and one by one removed them and put them in a separate pile. He was excessively careful. Periodically he showed us how he would remove a tiny card of microfilm and walk across the room with it and place it on Cass Boulding's desk.

I asked him how many times he copied the original thousand pages. His answer, fifteen. I asked him how long it took him to do this. Two weeks. Why so long? Mistakes were made, corrections had to be inserted. What was Cass doing this whole time? Sitting at his desk, sometimes listening to his tape recorder through headphones, sometimes writing with a pencil, sometimes typing. Typing what? Lots of different things, Chato didn't know for sure. Corrections of the material sometimes.

And one letter about twelve pages long. We gathered that Cass wrote it over and over again, and each time he did a new one, he burned the old one.

Did he make a microfilm of the letter?

No. He made fifteen Xerox copies of it—Chato pantomimed where the Xerox copier was—and put them into envelopes with the microfilms, which were taped together between cardboard.

"Do you know who the letters went to?" asked Jinks.

We gathered that Cass had told him they were going to newspapers all around the country.

Matt Gillette's plan. The briefcase the guard had slammed on my hand.

We had been talking for over an hour and Chato was sobering up enough so that I didn't have to ask one question for every answer. His mind was becoming lucid, and he was asking and answering his own questions in a steady stream of telling us what happened.

I expressed sadness that all the copies of the material had probably been destroyed, since none of the letters had been mailed.

Chato's eyes brightened and he smiled with cunning and hope. He reached into his shirt at his chest and, miming, pulled out an imaginary pouch and inserted something into it.

"The Apache bead pouch that your father gave him?" asked Jinks.

"Si. Yes."

"Dad is like that," she whirled and said to me. "He always keeps a safe copy of important documents. Is that what he was doing, Chato? Did he put an extra copy into the pouch?"

And as Chato was nodding his head, my one dealing with Cass as a live man was vivid in memory. In the construction trailer, he was poking himself in the chest and saying, "I have the answer right here," speaking intensely to Jinks. I had thought he meant he had the answer in his heart, which is what he wanted me to think when he looked at me, a total stranger, out of the corner of his eye. I had blundered into his life at a critical moment, and during those minutes he was telling me I was to get the hell out of his life, he must have been connecting: me to Matt Gillette, Sheila to me, and all of us to the forces trying to stop him from revealing the microfilmed material in the letters and in the pouch on his chest. And since he knew and loved Jinks too much to suspect her, he was trying to tell her in code to get me out of his way.

But why suspect *me*? Certainly he didn't suspect Matt Gillette. But me? He knew me only by reputation, as a Coyote, an investigator. Maybe he thought my motives were purely mercenary, that I was a hired gun who would work for whoever paid me. Or maybe he thought I had been working against Matt Gillette all along, while appearing to work for him. Cass Boulding certainly could have thought that with the number of bribes and loans he had paid over the years. He knew men were often not doing what they professed to be doing.

Beyond the closed door a commotion of Melba's and children's voices rose, and then above them came Claude Boulding's voice. We fell silent while Melba argued with him, and as I rose to go toward the door, it burst open. In it stood Claude Boulding, Les Skinner, Ralph Stark and other sheriff's deputies.

"Mother called me," Claude said to Jinks.

*"No diles nada,"* I said to Chato. *"Mataron a Cassandro. No diles nada."* I garbled my Spanish as much as possible, mumbling and almost swallowing the words as I spoke them so that Chato could understand but the others could not. Chato's eyes fastened on me and

widened as Ralph Stark sprang through the door and told me to shut my mouth.

Back in my truck, Jinks said, "You and Chato weren't speaking Spanish. Not the Spanish I know."

"Pachucho, a different dialect. It started as Spanish but was trampled by Pancho Villa's Yaquis and dragged thousands of miles across the desert behind slow wagons."

"Some things you said I couldn't understand at all. Not at all."

I hoped no one else had understood when I told Chato to keep his mouth shut because the men bursting into the room had killed Cass. It was the only thing I could think of to really silence him while they questioned him.

# Part Three

# 22

Mexican children were still playing in the streets as Jinks and I drove through the *barrio*. I was numb with dread as I realized I would have to wait until dark and then climb down into the well to retrieve the pouch from Cass Boulding's chest.

"Pull over," said Jinks. "I think I better show you something."

I swung into a parking lot and turned off the engine.

Jinks didn't look at me when she spoke: "You asked me if Joshua knew that Dad is not his real father. I lied. He knows. All this disgusts me so much I wanted to push it all out of the way. I didn't think it was important, anyway. But I don't know anymore. I don't know anything. I remember that Joshua wanted to know who his father was when he was in college. He was as crazy then as he is now. Then suddenly he wouldn't talk to me about it anymore, and soon after that he joined the marines. Then I didn't see him for a couple years.

... Anyway, that's not what I want to talk about. Dad is the important one now. He used to be what he seems to be, one of the brothers of Boulding Brothers. Then, in his forties, he started changing very fast, becoming the man I respect so much now. That's why Chato said Joshua and I made him better. But that's not true, he made himself better. . . ."

She reached into her purse and took out a plain white envelope and held it between us, not yet offering it to me.

"That first night after Dad's party, after you left my apartment, I found this in the large briefcase. It's a letter to Mom, but I don't think he ever mailed it or a copy. That is another way he clarifies his feelings, by writing letters to people but not mailing them. . . . I'm so confused now. I don't know what this has to do with anything, but it will help you understand Dad."

She handed me the letter.

Dear Sheila,
When all your subtle hints formed themselves into a whole certainty and I realized for certain that Joshua was not my blood son, I was ready to kill you. It would not have been a well-planned murder, had I done it; no, I was in too much of a rage for that. I remember sitting in the living room with you one night. Joshua was in high school. I complimented him for some work he had done. You said something and smiled—no, it was more a vengeful smirk than a smile—and from then on I knew, gradually more each day as I sifted through your previous smirks and sayings, that he was not my son. I forget your exact words (isn't it strange that I still cannot remember the

exact words that opened that terrible door) but they were something about my not taking too much credit for Joshua. But I do remember your tone. It conveyed more than your words anyway.

As my certainty grew during the following days, I sank into a rage and a depression which I thought would kill me, or you. Sometimes on awakening I would wander aimlessly about the house feeling that I had already killed you, opening doors into startlingly empty rooms. About that time, I think, you sensed you had let the cat out of the bag, because you became extremely kind toward me. You never passed by me in the house without some soothing words or caress.

You even asked me what was wrong, I remember, and I said something about trouble with a construction job.

When next you left for one of your trips to visit "relatives," I left on one of the "business" trips which became so frequent during the following years. In fact, I went to Mazatlán, where, I felt, there was less chance of my murdering anyone. I took a room in a cheap hotel (so I wouldn't run into any other pillars of Phoenix) and I drank. One night when I was sober enough to walk safely through the streets, I went to a whorehouse. I was not seeking love or even companionship, I now realize, but a kind of revenge. I regarded women as something lower than cockroaches (strange how I generalized this experience with you to include all women) and I wanted to be among the worst of cockroaches.

I intended to find the meanest, foul-mouthed whore I could find and then perform acts I can no longer remember, but when I entered the front door of the place, into the room where the women sat around half dressed and men, as at an auction, chose their meat, I

145

was stunned. In the corner of the room, off by herself, sat a young girl of maybe fifteen. Her eyes were moist and red from dried tears. She was about Jinks's age. In her posture I could see terror, as though she knew my evil thoughts and was crying until I arrived.

I had to turn and go out into the dark. When I returned she was still sitting in exactly the same position. I paid for her and we went to her room.

She turned out the light, she said, because she was ashamed. She had only seen her brothers naked and she asked me not to hurt her.

I turned on the light and begged her forgiveness. I asked her about her life. For a long while she stared into my eyes, then burst out with tears of joy and thanks to the Virgin for answering her prayers. She threw her little girl's arms around my neck and hugged me as a child hugs a father, then led me to her dressing table and had me kneel beside her and give thanks to a plaster icon of the Virgin.

She talked and I was bewildered. An hour earlier I was so filled with loathing I was sick, and now I was filled with desires to be the answers to her prayers. I attributed it more to my experience of her innocence and terror than to the invisible hand of the Virgin, but it was an experience I did not want to end. Somehow answering her prayers replaced murdering you as a way to make sense of my life. I did not understand it then, nor do I understand it now.

Her father had been sick the past winter, and she had come to Mazatlán to make money to send home. After several weeks of searching for work, she had that day succumbed to invitations to work in the house. She had walked through the same front door I walked through only hours before I did.

She chattered on about her father's farm and her

brothers who were too young to support the family and her father's illness, while the flickering light from the votive candle played over her girl's face. I was so touched by her total devotion to her family I leaned back on her bed and felt a lessening of that rage that had been driving me mad for weeks, and suddenly I was possessed of a love for her that was so fierce I reached out, gently, and brushed my hand over the side of her face. She cringed, slightly; I was, after all, sent by the Virgin, and it was her first night on the job. But then she seemed to remember something (perhaps what the other women had told her about her duties) and she kissed my palm.

I don't know where it came from, the exact electrical mechanics of the impulse, but suddenly I wanted to kill her. I had a gun in my pocket which I had been carrying since shortly after your comment and smirk opened the door, but it was not even the gun I wished to use. The weapons I really wanted to use were deeper, more animal, more personal. My teeth, my hands. And yet through it all one strand of sanity knew that this beautiful young Indian girl in no way deserved to be the victim of the insane angers and rages of the Phoenix Anglo aristocracy. Instead of killing her, I gave her a hundred-dollar bill, and as I did it I realized that helping her was really my deepest desire, deeper than my desire to kill her (which made no sense in any context). She thanked the Virgin profusely, dancing around the room on her toes, clutching the money to her breast. It seemed to me that this love, this caring for family, was the foundation of the world and that without her the world, my world at any rate, would dissolve. I gave her all the money I could find in my wallet (I think it was about a thousand) and I told her I was a crazy man. She told me that was not true, that I had been touched by the Virgin (she held the gold-framed picture in front of my face) and that what I was feeling was not insanity but a sort of ecstasy. I laughed bitterly at her, and she, being too innocent for sarcasm, laughed joyfully with me. In the end her joy deflated my bitterness.

We went on like that for hours, laughing and talking. She could not understand me, nor did I want to corrupt her by a detailed explanation of my experiences and feelings, but the joy and hope she felt from some cheap candles, a picture of the Virgin and a mere eleven hundred dollars was doing something good inside me. Her love for her family was infecting me.

Then suddenly, in the midst of all that terrifying good feeling, I became profoundly sleepy. I told her and she caressed my face. I fell asleep instantly and was dreaming that Chato's grandfather came into the room. I remembered him from the time I was about nine and he was over a hundred. He looked exactly as he had the times Chato and I would go to the old man's adobe hut, where he sat in the shade looking south with those dark eyes out of his eroded face. In the dream the old man, old Chief Emiliano Moseis, was lean and strong, and he took my hand and led me out into the night, where he turned into a raven. He flew away and I followed. I was intensely interested to see if I too had turned into a raven, but it was too dark to see my body. Below I could see scattered campfires and the outline of the Superstition Mountains in the moonlight, and as I flew I was buffeted by emotions, as a raven is knocked around by drafts of wind. Strong, pure emotion without many thoughts. Desires. Love for you followed by the desire to hurt you. Love for Joshua. Guilts, feelings, too many to name, but you can imagine. I could not recognize them all at the time, but the memory of them stayed with me, and during the following years I have been able to go back to that dream of flight and feel it again, and digest it a little at a time.

It was dawn when we landed in the mountains (I forgot to look to see if I was a raven in the light) and once we were on the ground he (a man again) was leading me up a red rock canyon with water in it. We hopped from rock to rock. The water rushing around the stones at our feet held thousands of fish of different colors. We came to a sheer walled canyon not much wider than my shoulders and had to wade through water up to our bellies running swiftly against us, but when we emerged from those sheer walls we were in an open lush valley, beneath the shade of giant cottonwood trees. To my right was a campfire, and men were sitting around it. He took me to one of the men, whom he said was to be my helper, and he told me to tell him what had hurt me. I told my helper you had slept with another man and that I had only recently found out that Joshua was not my own son. I talked and talked to him.

At last he raised his hand and said to me: "You talk about this woman and about the young man Joshua as though they were land or horses. Not even land or horses are yours. If you did not feel they belonged to you, you would not be in such a rage. You cannot love what you possess; you can only protect and control it. The spirit that gave us life gave us what we need to live. But you make yourself sick by feeling you own a woman or a child, or even a horse or a house. If they belong, they belong to the great spirit, and to remind us of this, the great spirit makes people and horses grow old and die and houses to crumble. Attach yourself to what is living, to love, and you will not be in such a rage and such a sickness."

That is what the old man said. I have not done justice to it here, because I cannot remember the exact words. I can't even remember if he spoke words. He may have just looked at me and caused me to feel, to think these words. And I realize there is a certain corny sound to the words, but there is a truth in them, too. I think probably that the cornier the words sound to any listener is a measure of the distance of that listener's understanding from the deeper meanings of life.

I am sure of this because when I woke the young girl was sitting in a chair next to the bed, watching me intently in the flickering candlelight. I was soaking in sweat as though I had just weathered a terrible fever.

I remembered every detail of the dream, and the impulse to kill her (which had been totally insane) never returned. Nor did the impulse to hurt you (which had been not quite totally insane).

The next few days were the beginning of my healing, to the extent that one who has lived my life can be healed. I realized right off that eleven hundred dollars might not be enough to solve her problems, and since I had decided I wanted to solve her problems to pay for my cure, we rented a car and drove to her family's house in the mountains. I talked to her father and to her brothers, took her father back to the city for medical attention and gave her the necessary money. I felt very good about it all. I had done something right.

When I returned to Phoenix, I wanted to shoot the other man, though I still did not know who he was, but I came to understand you. By understanding the position of the young woman I had helped (and did not use her, except that helping her helped me, too) I began to realize that when you and I were first married, I had just inherited a good portion of a four-hundred-thousand-acre ranch that is now west Phoenix. By comparison you were poor. I remembered our early fights, before either Jinks or Joshua were born. Shameful dialogues came back to me in which I used my wealth to intimidate you. Aside from the underlying reality that greed doomed us both, I had you between a rock and a cactus. In those days, the only career open to an ambitious woman like you in Phoenix was to be married to a man like me.

I realized all this from understanding the position of that young woman. She was in a position worse than a cow. Cattle are genetically selected, branded, dehorned and castrated by men, but they never are forced to pretend they like it. They are mistreated, but they don't fake pleasure and get paid for their fakery. And they don't develop the deep hatred that grows beneath smiling submission.

All this and much more came to me during painful flashes over the next years. Many times I tried to talk with you but you would have none of it by then. Your own guilt over your own crimes of passion was too much. You cried, screamed at me to shut up and left the house whenever I tried to sit down and talk this all out.

I fell into a different kind of anger toward you, and partially toward myself, one for which no dream has come to save me. Once I had given up owning Joshua, I loved him more. And once my eyes were opened to what had happened, I saw how the life you and I had lived had hurt him.

I have not been able to forgive myself for that, nor

have I been able to forgive you.

So we fell into those years of silence and mutual avoidance. Then finally I did what I had to do. For certain wounds inflicted on love there is no healing.

I'm telling you all this for selfish reasons. I have another very important project on my mind now, and I felt that if I wrote this all out it might clear some of my vital attention so that I might form a better future than my past has been.

I hope you can heal yourself, too.

Sincerely,
Cassandro

When I looked up from reading the letter, Jinks's eyes were moist. While working for Matt Gillette, I had badly wanted to snag Cass Boulding, and I had seen him as simply an evil man. Now I realized he was many things, but he was not simple. And I was glad he had made peace with his past before he was murdered. He didn't finish his present project, but he had made peace with his past.

"Is there anything else you're not telling me?" I asked Jinks.

"No." She sucked her lips and looked at my steering wheel.

"Do you know who Joshua's father is?"

"No."

"Does Joshua?"

"No."

"Does Sheila?" My voice was as full of sarcasm as my words. Jinks's eyes met mine for one moment of recognition and she was mad enough at me to spit.

"I'm sorry," I said. "But I'm tired of getting this in little bits and pieces. So you can ask your mother tonight who is Joshua's father. That will save her the embarrassment of my asking her in the morning."

"She'll fire you."

"That doesn't matter anymore. I'm working for myself now."

# 23

After I left Jinks at her place, I realized I had two things to do before I could get on with my life. One was a pleasure. The other I dreaded more than nightmares. First I had to feed Bandit, who had missed his dinner the previous day because I worked myself into exhaustion and slept on Jinks's couch. Then I had to go back to the well where I dumped Cass Boulding, climb down into it and retrieve the Apache bead pouch from around his broken neck.

The only sounds from Bandit before he rushed out of the darkness and leaped into the truck beside me came from his pads on the gravel road. At home I poured him a double ration of dog food. I went inside and ransacked my closet, searching for the flashlights and rope and pitons I would need to go down into the well and retrieve the microfilm. At first I cussed myself for not searching the pouch in the first place, then praised myself for putting Cass where I could find him again if I needed him. Had I left him by the side of the road somewhere, the microfilm would have disappeared as surely as all other unpleasant evidence in Phoenix when the authorities found him.

Though I had made mistakes, my instincts had been correct. Had Les Skinner gotten hold of Cass's body, the entire legal machinery of Phoenix would have slid into motion to arrest and convict someone, anyone, to give the public a simple and false answer to a larger, unanswered question. Since they had not been able to find Cass, they had not been able to cover up what really happened to him, because the national news media had remained fascinated with the fact that he was missing. Had he been found dead, they would have lost interest within a few days.

I heaved my gear into the back of my truck and climbed into the cab. Bandit lay on the seat beside me cringing, as though trying to make himself invisible in the darkness. He wanted to go with me and knew I would not let him.

"Out, Spot."

He whined. I pointed toward the open door and explained, briefly, why he could not come. Usually such an explanation would satisfy him, but he whined again.

"Don't make that sound. You know it makes my heart ache. Now, out! I've got to go do something very unpleasant and you've got to stay and guard the house."

Still he did not move.

"Come on, I mean it." I took hold of the scruff of his

neck and pulled him over my lap toward the open door. He jumped down and walked in a badly injured way to the front porch where he collapsed and watched me drive away, his eyes glinting out of the black patch around them.

# 24

Driving north at night, I saw another decision. I could either go climb down in the well with Cass Boulding, or I could drive into Mexico and never speak English again.

The thought of Mexico tugged at me, and I turned off the road to consider it. I would live in La Paz and become a fisherman and marry a Mexican woman without a drop of vicious European blood in her veins. At first I would be viewed with suspicion as an outsider, but soon my total immersion in their life would make me invisible. My Spanish was already fluent; I had only to learn their accent. I would never wear shoes again.

I began to feel the flow of my total immersion in my new life when I remembered Ray, a patient in a psychiatric ward where I once worked. He used to shuffle back and forth along the halls, and every time I tried to talk to him he glared defiantly at me and said, "You know nothing about my story."

"That's because you won't tell me," I said.

"It's too hot," he said. "Too hot." And he shuffled away. And he never did tell me, nor anyone else. One day after he was discharged he poured a quart of gasoline over his head and lit a match.

I turned off the ignition and the lights and ran into the desert. I dodged cactus and crashed through stinging mesquite brush until my head started to clear.

By the time I turned off on the road which led to Boulding's well I knew exactly what I had to do.

When I was far enough from the highway so my lights would not be seen, I got out and checked the tire tracks in the dirt. The tread marks matched mine, though they had been blunted by recent winds. Still my tracks were the most recent. No one had entered or left after I had dumped Cass.

I drove on over the desert wilderness road, acutely aware of the workings of my engine and transmission. Yellow eyes glittered in the road ahead and disappeared. A jackrabbit, caught by his own terror in the funnel of my headlights, ran along in front of the truck for a quarter mile before veering off into the night.

When I came to the well I did not stop moving for one instant. First I tied one end of my climbing rope to the bumper of my truck and dropped the unwinding coils into the hole in the ground.

My flashlight beam reached to the shiny black water in the square frame of rock fifty feet below. Out of the water rose an oak beam that had fallen from above and lodged in the shaft at water level. Floating in the shiny water were a dead rabbit and a roadrunner with its wings spread.

There was no sign of Cass Boulding, and there was no real indication of how deep the water was. My hope was that the beam slanting out of the water was resting on the bottom and that the beam itself was no more than fifteen feet long.

I stripped down, shivering in the night wind, and put on my backpack containing my diving mask, knife, underwater light, and pitons.

After testing the knot on the bumper and tying my climbing boots, I went over the side and began the long descent. The walls were five feet apart, and so I was able to descend in a crouch perpendicular to the wall down which my feet inched backwards. My breathing echoed weirdly in the rock enclosure, and small stones broke loose and fell to splash below.

And I tried not to think. There is a time to think and there is a time to act, and to dream about my wife and children and fishing boat in La Paz at that time was not safe. I realized I should be concentrating on my footholds but I could not see them. I needed the small flashlight I had in my truck. I could carry it in my mouth and spotlight each foothold. I was deciding to return to the top for the flashlight when a large rock under my right foot gave way and I slipped, then slammed full body into the wall. I bounced and dangled and the sliding rope burned my hands and back.

I pulled myself over the top and dug into the glove compartment of my truck and found my small flashlight.

Back over the edge, I felt a little safer this time, shining the light on footholds and then testing them before depending on them. I descended slowly.

The water was icy. When I was in up to my waist, I hitched my rope under my armpits and hung there while I lifted and twisted the end of the heavy oak beam that rose out of the water. It was so heavy I judged it to be about fifteen feet long, and when I turned slightly I could feel a grinding as though the bottom was resting on loose gravel. I was in luck.

Standing on the slanting beam, with my shoulder against one wall for support, I drove two pitons into the adjacent wall with my hammer. I was in this situation because I had become confused and not done my job correctly in the first place, and nothing was going to stop me from doing it thoroughly this time. I didn't want to retrieve the pouch this time only to find out later that Cass liked to keep his best secrets in his shoe.

From one piton I hung my backpack, tool belt and my boots. My jaws were aching from holding the small flashlight when I put it in the backpack and switched to the larger underwater light. Before I descended into the black water I scooped the decomposing rabbit and road-runner into the corner below the oak beam.

My first dive took me down no more than ten feet and I began to realize my task was not going to be as easy as it looked. Though only one beam protruded from the surface of the water, beneath that surface was a forest of railroad ties. Six feet beneath the surface one had lodged horizontally, and I had to swim down headfirst and keep it always in mind so that it would not trap me on my return trip. My flashlight would not penetrate the water more than a few inches, and I decided it was more trouble than it was worth.

At the surface again, I put the light into my backpack, deciding to feel my way to the bottom. Later when I had retrieved Cass, I could use my light to examine what I found.

Or so I decided with my head above the surface of the icy water, but when I was down at the level of the horizontal beam once again, I panicked and streaked blindly up.

Holding to my rope, I had time to reflect that another panic like that would kill me. Had I been below the horizontal beam and leaped headfirst into it . . . I could not afford to panic again.

Down again I went to the horizontal beam, feeling this time like a veteran. The beam was my home base in the darkness, and I pulled myself past it, descending and feeling all around with my free hand, still holding it, when I felt it let loose above me and begin to sink. With perfect clarity, I guided it past my rising body as I started to return to the surface, but I was caught. The barbed wire I had used to lower Cass Boulding into the well wrapped around me in the dark. One coil bound my right shoulder, and when I tried to muscle my way up, I found my right leg tangled in another. My panic told me to thrash my way to the top; my good sense told me I would only tighten the barbed wire if I moved without thinking. Then the wire not only held me, it began to tug downward, and for an instant I thought Cass Boulding had cast it up like a net and snared me and was now pulling me down with him.

Until I remembered the sinking beam and realized it had hit the tangle of wire. I kept telling myself the beam was pulling me down, and instead of trying to swim up, I turned and followed my snare, unwrapping it from my shoulder and my leg as I descended. One of my flailing hands found the root of a mesquite tree jutting out of the caliche wall, and I used it to pull myself still farther down. Then, emerging from the last of the coils of wire, I was free. I looped away and kicked up to the surface once again.

I rested and realized I was numb with the cold and wondered how much longer I could last. Not long. When I had my breath back I plunged headfirst downward into the darkness, keeping the barbed wire to my right, as though I meant this time to go all the way to the bottom.

Something brushed the back of my neck and I went insane for an instant then came out of it because I did not have time for it. Starting with his bloated hand, I traced Cass Boulding's body until I found his ankle with the rock tied to it with barbed wire. Unwinding the wire, my lungs were about to burst. Then his ankle was free and I heaved him toward the surface and swam around him, thinking my lungs had already burst as I came up out of the water.

I dangled from my rope and gasped until I could get the strength to remove my waterproof flashlight from the pack. Cass still had not surfaced when I turned it on, but I knew he would be along soon.

The light played over the black water and my breathing echoed and I was shivering uncontrollably. When Cass's head cleared the surface of the water no more than a foot from my face, I was not prepared for the sight of it.

He had turned white and had bloated to twice his normal bulk. I turned off the light and held onto the beam while I recovered.

Beneath his arms I tied the loose end of my climbing rope and threaded one end through the piton six feet above the water. I hoisted him up until only his feet were still in the water.

With one foot on the beam and the other on the vertical wall, I was able to stand in front of him. First I found the Apache bead pouch hanging from his neck and slid open the leather drawstrings. Inside was a wad of microfilm copies. I held one sheet up to the light and though I could certainly not read any of the microscopic lettering, I could see there was enough material in the pouch to fill a fat book. I put the pouch into my backpack then found his wallet and threw it in, too.

With my knife I cut the material of his sports jacket, searching for hidden pockets or other material in the regular pockets.

Most of Boulding's clothing was already in shreds caused when it split from the bloating. With my knife I removed the material piece by piece and examined it before throwing it behind me to let it sink once again.

I had removed the insole from his second shoe when I noticed I could see better. Too well. Sweat was pouring off my forehead into my eyes, and I wiped them with my forearm. Looking around I saw the entire bottom of the well around me was illuminated.

I looked up into a flashlight beam shining straight down on me like an interrogation-room light, and for an instant I saw myself as an innocent bystander, a camper, say, might see me, with my knife blade removing the insole of Cass Boulding's shoe, with his bloated lizard-belly-white body hanging on the wall in front of me.

The light went away and I was in total darkness again. I wanted to shout and explain but didn't know where to begin. Nor to whom I was explaining. The light came back again but this time there was a large black hole in the middle of it growing larger.

I ducked forward, hugging Cass Boulding, as a boulder streaked by my back and exploded in the water. No one had yet said one word, and I knew I was in for some terrible discomfort.

Feet first I plunged into the water and came up in a tiny corner beneath the slanting beam. My nose was covered with roadrunner carcass and feathers, and my forehead touched the bottom of the beam when another bomb hit the water.

It was a small space, and the waves were big. Under water I held to the walls so that the man with the light could not see me beneath the beam. The next rock hit the beam itself and glanced off to make waves. The roadrunner bounced around on top of my upturned face and the water lapped around Cass Boulding's ankles.

The light went away again as the silent one above went in search of more rocks, and I did not make a sound. My only hope was that he thought I was already dead at the bottom. If he saw me he could keep dropping rocks until I died of the cold.

The light came back and the next rock hit Cass and tore him loose from the piton. From my safe triangle I saw his white naked bulk topple forward and disappear beneath the surface. It was silent for a while and the light did not go away again. As quietly as possible I breathed the feathers and rotten flesh of the roadrunner.

Soon after the light went away again my climbing rope came falling in uneven coils. The light came back and I watched the rope slip beneath the surface. This time the light stayed on so long I was afraid I would black out from the cold.

Then it was gone for good. I waited, straining to listen, until I heard an engine start in the distance and drive away. I came out from beneath the beam and crawled onto it and listened to my clattering teeth.

When my shivering did not stop, I decided I'd better get to work or I would die. It was so dark I could not see anything, but I had come to know the bottom of this well so completely it didn't matter.

I had two alternatives, neither of them safe and neither of them pleasant. I could dive into the water again and retrieve my rope and tie one end to my hammer and throw it out of the well, hoping it would catch on something so I could pull myself out. But I couldn't bear the idea of going into the water again.

Or I could wedge myself out. The well was five feet on a side, and from my toes to my outstretched arms I'm about seven and a half feet long. Leaning forward off my beam, I fell until my palms caught the opposite wall. Straining out with every muscle, I stepped backward with my heels and walked forward with my hands.

The first fifteen feet were easier than I feared, but

then the muscle cramps came and I had to stop to rest. I found I could rest a shoulder on the third wall while I let loose with one arm and shook it. I ascended like that, resting at intervals, using the rest periods to nourish myself with thoughts of revenge.

After I hauled myself over the top I lay on my back panting and rubbing my arms. And I saw the sky for the first time in my life, deep blue and endless and salted with numberless stars. I saw Taurus and kissed him and kissed the ground and crawled over to my pickup and kissed the back bumper.

Driving out the dirt road, yellow eyes flashed and disappeared and, later, a jackrabbit was caught in my headlights. This time I did not continue at my same speed, waiting for the rabbit to jump out of the cone of my headlights. This time I stopped and turned off my lights and waited for him to hop away.

# 25

Now that I was safely dead, I figured I deserved a night's rest. I was still trembling with fear and rage, and now was not the time to call Matt Gillette and Joshua and Jinks together to try to sort out what had happened. Whoever murdered Cass was sure I was at the bottom of the well with him, and I was sure I could use the element of surprise to my advantage. But for the moment I was so tired I didn't want to think about it all for a while. All I wanted was to go home and sleep.

I turned onto the dirt road leading to my house and stopped the truck. I waited in the darkness with the door open for Bandit to leap into the cab, shivering with excitement to see me.

He didn't come even after I whistled, and I knew something was wrong.

Still more than half a mile from my house, I turned off the truck and took my flashlight and pistol and got into the desert as quickly as I could. There was enough moon for me to see the dark forms of cacti and brush, and I jumped down into an arroyo and hiked above my house. When I emerged from the thick brush of mesquite and paloverde, I was at my own back door.

Bandit was lying on his side on my back porch, with his head in a pool of blood. I knelt down and took his head and felt with my thumb a bullet hole between his eyes in the middle of his mask.

Someone had come for me, probably around midnight, judging from the warmth under Bandit's sleek hair. The man had sneaked up on my house only to find it empty, and he had forced his way in to wait for my return. Bandit had stood on the back porch barking at him until the man in the house opened the door and held his gun to Bandit's skull.

The white places on Bandit's fur gleamed in the moonlight as I removed my shoes and socks. I couldn't figure out why Cass Boulding's killer wanted me dead twice in one night. I readied my flashlight and pistol and crept up to my back wall.

Through my back window I could see my front door. Near it a man was waiting for me. He was sitting in one of my kitchen chairs and smoking. The gleam of his cigarette was the only source of light in the entire room. It rose and brightened as the smoker sucked on it, and I recognized the profile of Tony Scottsdale, an alias chosen by Anthony Faretta when he came to Phoenix three years earlier and stayed, saying that the climate agreed with him. I had been on good terms with the FBI at the time, and their records showed the man had executed at least twelve men before he left Detroit, and his methods would have made good bedtime reading for Hitler. Soon after he arrived in Phoenix, Matt Gillette's star witness in a land fraud case had been disposed of like Bandit.

Scottsdale snuffed out one cigarette on my cement floor and a moment later lit another one. The match flame lit him nicely, and before he blew it out I had fired through my back window and shattered his right elbow. He roared and sprang from the floor as I blinded him with the light and told him to lay face down and not move.

After I had his good arm handcuffed to one ankle and his shattered elbow wrapped in a towel, I threw him into a corner and questioned him. I threatened and yelled and cursed, but all he would say was, "I want to see my attorney." He knew that once I turned him over to the police he'd be out of jail within a couple of days. Killing a dog is not a crime in Phoenix. He also knew me well enough by reputation to know I would not kill him.

After I had badgered him for a while, the phone rang.

"That for you?" I asked him.

He tossed his head defiantly: "Tell 'em I'm tied up."

I picked it up and listened. Jinks was frantic: "Daniel! You all right?"

"More or less."

"Dan, I've been having these terrible feelings about you in danger. I've been so afraid. I've tried to call you all night."

"Jinks, I can't talk now. Is your brother there?"

When Joshua came on the line I said: "Joshua, if you can come to my house right now, I think you can help me find out what happened to your father."

He said he was on his way and hung up. I stared into Scottsdale's defiant glaring eyes and said: "Since you won't answer my questions, maybe you'd rather talk to the son of the man you murdered."

He thought exactly what I wanted him to think—that Joshua, in his rage, would not be bound by the same rules of interrogation as I was.

"I didn't kill him." A flat statement, no pleading at all.

"Like you weren't going to kill me."

"Let's be honest," he said. "I was going to hit you but . . . well, you see what happened. I don't know what happened with this Boulding. I was supposed to hit him the day after his party, but he disappeared. Then the guy I work for he tries to pay me, and I gotta be honest, and I tell him I don't hit this Boulding. I don't know what happened. I tell him I don't hit someone if he disappears."

"So the same guy who wanted you to hit Boulding tells you to kill me like a dog?"

"Maybe same guy."

"You want to tell me his name or you want to tell it to Boulding's son."

"I want to tell it to my attorney."

"We'll wait for Joshua."

"I tell you the guy disappeared. Nobody knows where he went."

"Somebody does. Now shut up."

A while later Joshua came in, gave me one look with his wild sleepless eyes and blinked spasmodically. I told him Scottsdale had killed Bandit, had tried to kill me and might have killed Cass. I didn't tell him about Cass

Boulding's body showing up in the back of my truck and about the incident with the well earlier because there wasn't time to explain my complex motives in keeping all that a secret. Joshua was already half crazed with grief and anger, and I didn't want to take the chance of him turning against me.

He listened to me, staring all the while at Scottsdale, before he sat down in a kitchen chair and buried his face in his palms.

"You better get me to a hospital, I might bleed to death," said Tony Scottsdale.

"Yeah, you might," said Joshua.

Scottsdale watched him, his hard eyes calculating.

Joshua rubbed his face with his palms for a long while. His already deep-set eyes seemed to have retreated another inch into his skull. He was looking at the world out of tunnels. I wanted to give him time to digest the situation before suggesting he and I go outside where I would mention to him that he could possibly scare Scottsdale into talking.

But Joshua broke. He said, "This makes me sick," and staggered out the front door into the night.

Scottsdale knew what I was thinking, and the shadow of a smirk crossed his face. "The police," he said. "Call the police."

I was glaring at Scottsdale when Joshua emerged through the front door with a twelve-gauge shotgun aimed at my face.

"I want you to handcuff your hands behind your back," he told me.

"Josh, that's not . . ."

"I'll blow your kneecaps off, Dan. Now, do what I say."

When I was handcuffed and safely on the couch, Joshua turned to Scottsdale, who was still showing no fear. He dragged him up off the floor and shoved him down in my kitchen chair. Scottsdale winced with the pain from his shattered elbow but otherwise showed no emotion. Joshua went to my kitchen sink and picked up a hunting knife my father gave me when I was a child. He tested the blade with his thumb and turned to me.

"This thing is dull, Daniel. Where do you keep your sharpener?"

"I'm not part of this," I said.

"No matter," he said and rummaged through drawers until he found a sharpening file. He gave the knife several deft strokes, felt it again and walked over to Scottsdale. The lines around Scottsdale's eyes seemed like they were carved in marble, but otherwise he showed no fear.

"Mr. Scottsdale, you came to my friend's house tonight to kill him. You did kill his dog, and you were hired to kill my father. Now I'm not even going to ask you who hired you for all this work; I want you to tell me without coaxing."

Scottsdale glared at me and showed no sign of having heard Joshua.

"Antonio, did you hear me?" Joshua's voice suddenly sounded like Gracious Boulding's—high-pitched, ancient, angry and full of mockery. The broad expanse of skin between my shoulder blades became electrified, but

Tony Scottsdale did not even hear Joshua's change in tone.

"Antonio, you didn't *hear* me," said Joshua, and with one motion took hold of Scottsdale's left ear and sliced it off at its roots.

Scottsdale's head whipped around as he tried to see around the side of his face to know if the disembodied ear in Joshua's hand was really his own. At first where the ear had been was a white gash which quickly turned red. And from the startlingly empty roots where the ear should have been sprung a series of tiny jets of blood, squirting rhythmically across the kitchen table.

Joshua said: "And then Simon Peter took out his sword and cut off the ear of the High Priest's servant. Then Jesus told Peter to sheath his sword, and Jesus touched the man's ear and healed him."

Joshua held the bleeding ear in front of Scottsdale's amazed eyes and said, "So, Mr. High Priest's servant, my quick move there only cost you one ear, but it cost me my soul. Jesus is no more, you killed him, so he can't heal your ear. You know what a soul is, Antonio?"

Scottsdale was still trying to see around the corner of his face to find out if the ear in Joshua's hand really had been his.

"Do you know what a soul is, Tony? Can you hear me?"

Scottsdale suddenly heard him and said he knew what a soul was.

"But you don't have one," said Joshua, his voice still high-pitched, maniacal and mocking. "Nor do I, anymore. My soul is squirting out of me right this minute, like your blood here. It's leaking out to stain Dan's floor. Now that was a pretty high price to pay for hurting you, and there's no real pleasure in it anyway. And I suppose I had other choices. I could have been stupid and called the police, but we know what would have come of that in Phoenix. Or I could have simply walked away and figured 'bad choice I made for a father there to get himself murdered.' Or I could do what I am doing to get the answer from you to the question I have not even asked, nor do I want to ask. But I will have the answer. My soul has gone to hell and my life won't last the week, Tony Scottsdale, so you figure it out: I've got nothing to lose. I hope you don't make me keep at this until I start to enjoy it. Dan, where do you keep your spoons?"

"Spoons?" said Scottsdale.

"What do you want spoons . . ."

"Just tell me where to find your spoons, Dan."

"I'm not having anything to do—"

"No, I'm sorry, Daniel. You're right. I won't ask you." He moved into the kitchen area and pulled open drawers until he found the silverware and pulled out two tea-spoons. He returned to the kitchen table and took up the file and gave it quick strokes across the tip of one of the spoons. He took a couple of minutes getting that one the way he wanted it, then he started on the other one.

"Let's be honest," said Scottsdale and fell silent, watching the file blade scrape filings off the spoon tip.

"Do you *see* what I'm doing?" said Joshua.

Scottsdale moaned, and one of the tiny jets of blood from his ear increased its spurting.

"It's so nice that you see what I'm doing, Antonio. I was beginning to think you could neither hear nor see. You seem to be all mask and no emotions, Antonio. Tell me, do you think much about a man you are going to kill for money? Do you think about his wife? His daughter? His son?"

"I didn't hit your father, to be honest."

"That wasn't really my question," said Joshua, putting the last few strokes on his second spoon. "Now let's be honest, Antonio. You know what the question was now, don't you? That's right. Now you've got no time to wait before you answer me." He took a spoon in each hand and rose.

"See what I mean, Antonio?"

"Jack Romulus," said Antonio, and his shoulders sagged.

"Is he being honest, Daniel?"

"That fits," I said. "Romulus had dealings with him before. I think Romulus brought him to Phoenix in the first place. There were seven murders we were gradually tracing toward Romulus when Matt Gillette lost the election."

"Do you know why?" Joshua asked Scottsdale.

"I never know why. I don't ever want to know why. Only how is all I ever want to know."

"*Vámanos,*" said Joshua and heaved Scottsdale to his feet and shoved him toward the door.

Joshua carried his shotgun under one arm and Scottsdale's pistol in his pocket, and my knife in one fist. When I asked to have the handcuffs removed, he told me no. In my shirt pocket was the one remaining bundle of microfilm pages, the last copy of the work Cass Boulding died for. I didn't know all the technical details on the microfilm, but after listening to Cass's diary, I was sure the most important thing I could ever do in my life would be to make duplicates of the microfilm and send them out, with a cover letter, to newspapers around the country, as Cass Boulding had tried to do.

As crazed as Joshua was, I could not predict what he would do if I told him. But I had to take the chance.

"Joshua, leave me here. You don't need me."

"Afraid I do, Daniel. This one here, I'll need to ask him some more questions. And Romulus. I'll need the use of your memory to tell me if they're lying."

"Joshua, your father is dead," I said. I thought of several lies I could have told but knew that Joshua, hypersensitive as he was, would hear them in my voice or see them in my eyes and then he would have been carving on me.

"I thought he was," he said. His face showed very little emotion, but he went over to a pine-paneled wall and began stabbing at it with my knife. Scottsdale stood slumped next to the front door. The thin jets of blood from the stump of his ear had coagulated.

"How do you know he's dead?"

Again I thought of lying, but decided it was too dangerous. So I told him everything. The first time I saw Cass's body while Jinks was hugging me. My feeling that I had been set up. My attempt at putting him under the culvert near Superstition Trail which was thwarted by a deputy. My crazed and careless dumping of him eighty miles north of Phoenix. My return earlier that night to retrieve the beadwork pouch containing the microfilm. My own silent murder. It didn't feel good telling all that to Cass Boulding's son.

"Where's the pouch?"

I pointed with my chin toward my shirt pocket. He came and removed it and the look on his face said he believed all I had said for the first time. His eyes flared and his jaw shot forward and the knife came up, vibrating in his hand.

To keep him from forgetting that I was his friend, I said, "You're scaring me, Joshua."

He lowered the knife.

I gave him a little more time to calm down before I said, "Your father's most important life work is in that pouch. I think we should make sure it gets into the right hands before going on with whatever you have in mind."

"What's on these?" he demanded, waving the microfilm in my face.

"A copy of all the material that was in the small briefcase Jinks and I found in the construction trailer the night Cass—"

"The meat, Dan! Hurry, I don't have long to live."

"I'm not sure."

"Guess."

"All the cheats that went on all the time. Short work. Cass had worked with the other contractors before, and he, better than anyone, knew the thousands of ways they cheat on plans. He tolerated it when they were building roads and subdivisions, but making a faulty nuclear power plant . . ."

"That's enough. I've got the picture."

"So let's get these to the right people, and carry out your father's plans."

"My plans first," he said and grabbed me by the ear and shoulders and shoved me forward. I crashed into Scottsdale as Joshua opened the door and shoved us out into the night.

# 26

Joshua drove my truck and Scottsdale sat between us. My hands were still cuffed behind my back. Scottsdale kept passing out, and I had to use my left shoulder to keep him from slumping forward onto the floor.

We had been bouncing over dirt roads for some time when I decided to speak to Joshua, using a technique I had learned while working in the psychiatric ward.

"Are you really as crazy as you're acting?"

"Worse," he answered, his voice normal for the moment. "But every time I close my eyes, even for an instant, I see snakes. If I didn't know exactly what I'm doing, it would be time for the straitjacket. I don't even like to think what I would have done if he hadn't given me Romulus's name when he did."

I had a hunch that if I could jolt him into a deeper awareness of what he was feeling, we might all come out of it alive. I asked: "You made your voice sound like your grandmother's when you questioned him. Did you do that for effect?"

"None of your goddam business," he said, and without any warning cuffed me across the face with the back of his hand. In the predawn darkness, with my ears ringing, I thought I was listening to Gracious Boulding.

A while later Joshua's voice was his own again. "You know," he said, "to the Hopis, snakes are messengers. When they do their snake dance they are giving the snakes messages to carry underground to the gods. The messages are prayers for renewal, rebirth. After the dances in autumn, the snakes go underground to the gods and ask that the gods not forget to return in the spring. And the gods have never yet forgotten. When spring comes the snakes emerge from the ground again."

"I didn't know that," I said. I wanted to keep him talking rationally.

"The snakes I see are not the same snakes the Hopis see," he continued. "My snakes are European snakes. And the way I see them is sick. Did you know that the sins of man are visited on his sons by their mothers?"

"No, I didn't know that."

"Claude, my uncle, you know him, sees the desert only . . . no, he doesn't see it, hear it. All he sees is open space which stirs in him the desire to crush and mutilate. That's what he gets paid for."

"What do you mean?"

"You know what I mean," said Joshua. "You're only trying to engage me in reasonable conversation. . . . It's rule one for dealing with maniacs. I did it hundreds of times when I was a medic. But I like you anyway, Daniel.

I'll try to keep you from getting hurt."

He turned off the dirt road and shifted into low gear and drove up the middle of a narrow arroyo between thick overhanging mesquite. When he came to a barbed wire fence spanning the wash he did not even slow down. The wires sprang taut and screeched and snapped like banjo strings and we went on, deeper into the narrowing dry stream bed. Once out of sight of the main road, after rounding a small meander, he stopped.

We were on the edge of Jack Romulus's horse ranch, twenty miles from downtown Phoenix. I knew the place well because I had staked it out for a month once to find a connection between Romulus and Scottsdale. Joshua knew the house and surrounding ranch, he told me, because Boulding Brothers Construction had built Jack's house.

Joshua got out and stalked off into the desert. Bulging from his pocket was Scottsdale's execution gun. Joshua had tested it as we walked out of my house, fired into the air, and the noise it made was no louder than the breaking of a small dry stick.

My hands were cuffed behind my back and my left leg was tied to Scottsdale's right leg.

Though there was no sign of the sun on the horizon, the desert was starting to grow lighter when Joshua returned. He flung open my door and slashed the rope tying Scottsdale and me together with my knife. He didn't say a word as he flung me out of the truck onto my face in the sand, then reached in and slapped Scottsdale awake. I wasn't sure if he was going to be able to stand up and walk. Blood from his shattered elbow and ear stump had drenched his clothes and poured down over the floor of the truck to drip out under the door.

As we covered the half mile to Jack Romulus's house, the light behind the Superstition Mountains brightened. The dawn was yellow and black and gray. Every time Scottsdale fell down, Joshua kicked him, breathing heavily, until the man was on his feet again. I watched the look in Joshua's eyes and realized that if I fell down I would receive the same treatment.

We came into a large grassy backyard, well shaded with mock orange trees, and walked around a large swimming pool. On Jack Romulus's back porch a man in green silk pajamas lay face down on the red cement. I couldn't remember his name, but he had arrived in Phoenix with Scottsdale and had worked as Romulus's bodyguard ever since.

Jack Romulus himself was tied hands and feet to one of his kitchen chairs. Joshua shoved me to the floor in a corner and sat Scottsdale down in a chair facing Romulus.

Joshua said, "Mr. Scottsdale, is this the man who hired you to kill my father?"

Staring at Jack Romulus, Tony Scottsdale suddenly had a lapse of memory and was silent.

Joshua took the sharpened spoons out of his pocket and laid them on the table beside him.

Tony answered his question.

"Tell me why, Jack. Don't you like the way he built your house?" Gracious Boulding's voice again.

The sky was now red with morning light and Jack

Romulus's eyes darted back and forth, unable to rest anywhere. He was silent.

"You don't seem to hear me very well, Mr. Romulus. So I'll tell you what. We're going to play a little game. Originally it was known as Christianize the Indians, then as Rape the West. Now it has a new name: Dog Eat Dog. I'm going to ask you a question, and if you don't answer or if you lie, I'm going to cut off something and feed it to Mr. Scottsdale."

He reached into his shirt pocket and withdrew Scottsdale's ear and pressed it to Jack Romulus's lips. Romulus gagged and looked with terrified amazement into Joshua's eyes.

"Don't tell me," said Joshua, mocking, "you are not a violent man. An ounce of meat makes you sick, yet you think nothing of killing a man. Jack, you've been playing Dog Eat Dog for years. All I've done is bring the rules out in the open. Now start chewing his ear or lose your own."

Jack Romulus said, "The nuclear thing. Cass Boulding was about to ruin it for us all. He had all this shit on microfilm he was going to send to newspapers. The money people thought it would be bad for the economy."

"So you hired Mr. Scottsdale to stop him?"

"Yes."

"Who are the money people you talk about?"

Romulus paused.

"Dog Eat Dog," said Joshua and raised the ear.

Jack Romulus listed ten men, and I was shocked. With all the investigative work I had done for Matt Gillette, even I didn't know six of them.

"And did Mr. Scottsdale kill my father?"

"That part I don't know," said Romulus. "And I'm not lying. Boulding disappeared a day before the hit date, but when I went to pay Antonio, he wouldn't take the money. He said he didn't know what happened to your—to Boulding."

"I'm an honest man," said Scottsdale.

"Then my father might still be alive," said Joshua.

"I think he is," said Jack Romulus.

"I know he isn't," said Joshua. "And I don't think you're telling me everything. Start chewing."

Jack Romulus gagged and flung his head to one side saying, "There's one more. One more I didn't tell you about."

"Who's that?" said Joshua.

"Your uncle."

"He paid?"

"Yes, he paid. He's one of the eleven."

Joshua took several steps backward and sat straight down on the floor. For a while he did not move. Then in a trance he began stabbing the floor with my knife.

I realized Claude Boulding was a man who did things for himself, and I saw the twin tire ruts swerving off the Boulding ranch road into the desert and Cass Boulding's broken neck that did not bleed. I saw Cass driving to his birthday party in the dark, talking to his brother, as something was said between them which caused Claude to flare up and leap from his seat to grab Cass Boulding's head and bend it over the top of the seat and heave all his weight onto it as the car swerved off into the desert and the spine at the base of Cass Boulding's skull

184

snapped. Then Claude, realizing what he had done and heaving his brother into the trunk of the car, drove on to the party in the darkness. Claude Boulding still stunned and not knowing what he was going to do until he saw my truck parked on the road. And Sheila Boulding clairvoyantly in touch with Cass, feeling the snap in her own neck, too, at the party, though not knowing what she felt and shrugging it off as an illusion. Then Claude coming into the party and squatting down by the fire next to Joshua and me, and beginning to realize that he himself had done the day before what Scottsdale was going to do for pay. But realizing that he had had to do it that way, because Cass had let it slip that he was going to disappear, kidnap himself right after his party to heighten publicity surrounding his revelations. Only Claude knew to watch me and follow me to the well the night before. It was Claude quietly jacklighting me like a rabbit in the bottom of the well as he aimed a boulder at my head.

Joshua quit stabbing at the floor with my knife and stood up.

I spoke for the first time since entering the house, "I don't think he's lying, Joshua, though a jury should decide that. Remember those twin ruts going off into the desert on your family's ranch road—"

"I saw them," said Joshua. "I see it all, now."

# 27

Joshua was driving the county dirt roads fast enough to kill us. The sun shot its rich red light over the shadowed desert, and my truck rose to the top of a rise and then plummeted down into the next arroyo. Rocks and sand drummed against the metal bottom.

I would not say anything to him about the speed because I was afraid he would kill me. After he got the information he wanted from Jack Romulus, he had pushed me outside and left me standing near the swimming pool and returned to the house. He was holding Scottsdale's silenced pistol when he entered, and an instant later I heard a sound like a stick breaking, and an instant later another similar sound.

"What shocks you most was that I did not get paid for killing them," Joshua said, suddenly whirling to look at me. He was driving much too fast to take his eyes off the road even for an instant, and I stared straight ahead at the scenery hurtling toward us to give him a hint. "Isn't it?" he insisted.

My hands were still cuffed behind my back, and I said yes to satisfy him. He looked back to the road.

"Cass Boulding was a saint," he went on, speaking more to the desert than to me. "He was not my father, but he was a saint. I'll bet you thought Joseph, husband of Mary, was the most saintly cuckold in history, but he wasn't. Cass Boulding was. Joseph thought that Jesus was conceived in Godly love, but Cass knew I was conceived in brotherly hatred. And yet he put all that behind him and loved me because I needed love, as all children need love and need not to be brought into feuds conceived before they were born. I can hear you wondering, Daniel, why don't I follow in his footsteps. Why don't I aspire to saintliness? I want you to know I did, at one time; enough to read of it, dwell in it . . . spend my time in the wilderness receiving my visions. But one of the worst visions I had was that America only respects violence. Saints are not seen as the wisest of men, which they are, but as fools. Gentleness is mistaken for weakness, violence and treachery for strength.

"That's why, now that I am finishing my father's work, I did not want to do anything that could be misinterpreted. Killing those two men back there was necessary because I am trying to make public the private life of nuclear energy. It's my own individual doom that in the process I will have to lay bare the relativity of relatives and kill my blood father to avenge the death of my spiritual father."

187

"Are you talking about your uncle?"

"About my father, about Claude Boulding. He engendered me in hatred and left the loving and raising of me to his brother."

"And your mother, do you think he forced her?"

"The other way around, I think. She was mad at Cass and used sex with his brother to punish him, at least in the beginning. Jinks told me that, and I believe it happened, though the deeper emotional mechanics of it are still a mystery to me. After I was born, Mother became confused. She began by using Claude as a weapon against her husband but grew confused so that she did not know which man she loved. And so grew to hate them both. This all did not happen in one house, in one city. There is not enough room in the largest castle for all that. It took two cities, Phoenix and Las Vegas. Cass ran the Phoenix branch of Boulding Brothers, and for fifteen years Claude ran the Las Vegas branch."

I had to keep him talking. I asked: "Did Jinks show you Cass's unmailed letter to your mother?"

"What's so strange is that letter didn't surprise me. All that stuff happened when I was about sixteen. I didn't know what was going on, but things were awfully weird around the house then. I remember several months when Dad walked around in a total daze. He couldn't even look at me for a long while, and when he looked at Mother I was afraid. But then he had that dream, and he grew to such a level of understanding that he even forgave her for what she had done by knowing her so deeply he understood she had to do what she did, given the people they were."

188

"You're saying that the tricks she played on Cass made him a better man?"

"Or it could have turned him into a killer or it could have broken him. He took the sudden plunge of insight and made himself into a better man with it."

"How do you know all this?"

"All the time Jinks and I were not with you we were listening to Dad's diary and talking and comparing a lifetime of impressions. Once we had ripped the mask off the family, the details soon followed."

"Why didn't you tell me?"

"It was none of your goddam business!"

I stared straight ahead at the oncoming road and Joshua, taking my hint, did the same. We turned onto the road leading to Claude Boulding's ranch when the sun was just above the peaks of the Superstition Mountains.

"About Cass's saintliness," I said. "What about the time your mother woke up in time to catch his fist before it hit her face."

"If he hadn't wanted her to catch it, she wouldn't have," said Joshua.

As we rounded the last curve before Claude Boulding's ranch house, I understood why Sheila had wanted to hire someone to protect her ex-husband. If she could sleep next to Cass Boulding and read his feelings and dreams, there was no reason she could not do the same while sleeping next to his brother.

# 28

"Uncuff me."

"Shut up."

"You're going to get me killed, you bastard."

Joshua was laughing maniacally. "You called me a bastard. Say it again. Truth feels good."

"Uncuff me."

"Shut up."

"Then pull off into the desert and tie me to a tree. But don't take me into this with my hands cuffed behind my back."

"Shut up," said Joshua. "I'm thinking."

"What are you going to do about Ralph Stark?"

"Shut up," he said, and put the point of my knife against my ribs.

Joshua was not thinking too clearly, or else he would not have pushed me in through the front door and followed. After a while Claude Boulding emerged into the living room from a long dark hallway. In one swift glance he saw Scottsdale's blood on my left arm, and he saw the gun in Joshua's hand. He didn't seem to notice my hands were cuffed, and the surprise at seeing me alive registered only in a convulsive lurching of his throat. Quickly he brought that under control by setting his teeth. His jaw muscles knotted.

"Tell me, Dad.... That's the first time I ever called you Dad," said Joshua, his voice shrill with notes of Gracious. "Tell me, so I can know if I've got it right. My Uncle Cass was driving to his party. You were sitting next to him. He said something that made you mad, and you lunged at him. The car veered off the side of the road into the desert and plowed to a stop. Uncle Cass's head was against your shoulder and you pushed it over the back of the seat. If you had let off then you would have given him only a bad whiplash, but you threw all your weight on it. He couldn't move and his neck snapped. You were no more than half a mile from the house. It was dark. You put him in the trunk, but when you got to the party you saw Daniel's truck and loaded him in."

"That's not quite how it happened," said Claude.

"How did it happen, Dad?"

"Can I sit down?" I asked. Ralph Stark would be in the room with us soon, and when it all broke loose, I wanted to be able to roll onto the floor and pray. Joshua ignored me, so I sat down in a nearby chair.

"Answer my question."

"We have a lot to talk about," said Claude.

"Sure, Dad. Answer my question."

"Where's Stark?" I asked.

"Shut up," said Joshua. He kept Scottsdale's pistol aimed at Claude.

"You know, Dad," said Joshua, his voice snarling. "It feels now like I knew it all along. When I was a kid and you used to look at me I felt something was wrong."

"Your mother and I," said Claude. "It can't be explained so quickly."

"Try," said Joshua, and that was the last thing he said. A plate glass window broke before I heard the shot, and I spun around to watch the instant round and still bloodless hole in the side of Joshua's head, and him falling to the floor, lurching and kicking like a shot deer.

Ralph Stark came in the front door and looked first at Joshua, then at Claude Boulding. "I didn't know what else to do," he told Claude.

Claude wore an emotionless mask. He reached up and rubbed the side of his face, examined the shaving cream on his hand and wiped it on his pants.

Ralph Stark grinned at me. The air whistled through his smashed nose. He said, "We got to figure out what happened, then put this one where he should be so the story fits."

The way things had shaped up, there was no sense in asking for my life.

Claude walked over and reached out for the pistol from Ralph. He said: "It pisses me off when I don't do something right. I already killed Falconer last night, dammit, but this time I want to do it right."

"If you don't mind," said Ralph.

"I mind." Claude reached for the gun and Ralph handed it to him reluctantly.

Through the broken window I saw the mountains sloping down into the foothills around us. The shadows of the jojoba and paloverde made tiny dark spots amid the rich colors of the morning light, and the hillside bathed in all its rich colors rushed in at me as I saw out of the corner of my eye Claude's hand, holding the pistol, rise to my skull height. I saw the beach and the ocean from my front porch in La Paz, and my tiny naked bronze children playing, and I had my arm around my Indian wife to whom I'd never spoken one word of English. And then I was pulling the fishing net into my boat as silvery fish leaped and slapped the sides and the blazing light off the water was so rich . . .

I heard the explosion but felt nothing. I looked down at my knees and waited for them to buckle, then turned to see Ralph Stark fall next to Joshua. He jerked around for a moment and then was still.

"I could have talked Joshua out of it," said Claude to Ralph's body, and then he said it to me. "With time Josh would have understood I did what I had to do." His voice pleaded with me to believe him.

"Probably," I said.

"This is all so disgusting," said Claude. The muscles in his throat tightened as though he was sick to his stomach.

"I think you could have talked him out of it," I said.

"You must have a hard head," said Claude. "I didn't want it to come to this."

"Me neither."

Claude knelt down over Joshua, facing away from me. For the first time I heard something like real emotion in his voice as he spoke to his dead son.

"Cass poisoned you against me. There was nothing I could do from Las Vegas. I tried. I took the Las Vegas jobs to get away, and when she would come to me I asked her to leave him and marry me, to bring you there where we three could start again. She went back to Phoenix, always went back. Then Jinks was born. I counted the months and asked her why she had cheated on me. She had told me she never loved him, never slept with him. She said he forced her, that one time she was pregnant with Jinks. She said she could not leave him while she was pregnant. She saw how mad I was at him for forcing her and she told me not to be so mad, to understand him. She was married to him and she said he had a right to expect.... He forced her, she said. After Jinks was born she didn't come up to see me for three years. I was crazy with grief. I distracted myself with work and women. There are lots of women in Las Vegas. Then she came back and told me.... It doesn't matter what she told me, they were all lies, anyway. They were only so convincing because she ... believed them, too."

Claude took Joshua in his arms and hugged him, weeping bitterly.

"After the divorce, she said she would marry me. She said she would explain everything to you so that you would understand and love me. She promised me. She kissed my face and eyes and held me so hard she was shaking and told me our life could begin finally.... Why was I a fool for so long?"

I was half listening to Claude; the rest of me was trying to clear my head of the wave of giddiness I felt when he killed Ralph instead of me. I knew that it would not take him long to come out of his grief long enough to kill me, burn the microfilm and concoct a story about how Joshua and I had killed Stark and Stark had killed us.

His sobbing quieted and he lowered Joshua's body to the floor. I stepped quietly to one side and saw him remove the microfilm sheets from Joshua's shirt pocket. I was up on my toes like a soccer player when he looked up at me. We were six feet apart. I could not move with him watching me. I had one chance, and if I missed it, I would be dead.

He said, "I thought these were why you went down into the well, you bastard. Why didn't you turn him in that first night?"

"I was too scared."

"That would have made it all so easy."

"Not for me."

"All this could have been avoided," waving his hand over Joshua.

"I'm sorry, I liked Joshua, too."

Still watching me, Claude took out his cigarette lighter and flicked it under the wad of microfilm. The center of the film bulged up from the heat, then burst into flames which ate toward the edges. As the flame neared Claude's fingers, I shifted my weight forward onto the balls of my feet. When he felt the flame he looked down and I sprang.

I had already gauged my first two steps and my kick. Claude saw me coming out of the corner of his eye and turned, startled, as the toe of my shoe caught him under the chin. He lurched back, falling, spitting blood and teeth, and not being able to use my cuffed hands for balance, I tripped over Joshua.

I fell to the tiled floor and saw Claude rise up to his knees and sit dazed still spitting blood and tooth chips. He wiped his mouth with the back of his hand. Without arms it was difficult to rise. I pulled my knees up under me and lurched around for balance. Claude put his hands on the floor and started to stand, but he was still so dazed his knee buckled and he fell back down. If he got to his feet I would not be able to kick him again and he would kill me.

I was lurching around like an armless lizard trying to get my toes positioned under me and my thighs coiled when Claude stood up. He had Scottsdale's gun in his hand and was still shaking his head and spitting when I sprang.

The top of my head hit the bottom of his jaw and as he was falling backward he raised the gun and fired. I saw the smoke but didn't hear the sound as I leaped and came down on him with both heels.

The microfilm was a curled ash and two tiny triangular corners that had not burned. I put my ear to Joshua's chest and heard nothing. I sat on the floor with my back to him and dug around in his pants pocket until I found the key to my handcuffs.

After my hands were free I put the cuffs on Claude. Then I locked him, still unconscious, in a closet, and I cut the telephone wires before I left.

# 29

I climbed over the back wall into Jinks's garden and looked through the sliding glass door. She sat curled up in a blue flannel nightgown in an easy chair. Through her fingers fretted a silver necklace chain. In a chair next to her Larry was asleep, his head thrown back over the top of the chair, his mouth wide open.

Stepping over Joshua's sleeping bag, I slid the door open. She looked up, startled, and ran to hug me, but when she saw my face she backed away.

"Why?"

"Back doors are safer."

Larry snorted, swiveled around in the chair and looked at me. He didn't say a word. Jinks sat back down and watched me, her hands fretting with the chain like a rosary without beads, a prayer without hope.

"What happened?" she asked, and cringed.

I told her, very briefly, without details, that Claude had killed her father and Ralph Stark had killed Joshua,

Neither of them asked what happened to Claude and I didn't say.

Every minute spent in Phoenix was bringing me closer to Skinner's control, and if I had not felt so much affection for Jinks, I wouldn't have stopped at her apartment. Telling her what happened was the most painful thing I have ever done, but I felt it was kinder for her to hear it from me than from Skinner and from newsmen. Their slant would twist and distort it and maybe destroy her.

Her reaction was silent. She folded her arms over her breasts and put her forehead on them. She was curled up in the overstuffed chair like a child. The only words she said were, "Daddy . . . Joshua . . . Daddy . . . Joshua . . ." She repeated the names over and over. I knew she was chanting these sounds to penetrate a wall of resistance, disbelief that was rising in her, and I knew that when this chanting broke through that wall she would fall into a deep and wailing grief. I wanted to stay and comfort her, but I had to save my life.

Because she could no longer hear me above her chanting, I told Larry I would write to her after her mourning and provide whatever information she needed to clear up this terrible mess.

"Take care of her," I said as I was leaving.

"I'll try," he said. "I'm not much good . . ." He paused and looked down at his flaccid hands. "But I'll have to get better. I'll try."

# 30

I went home and buried Bandit on a small delta in the dry wash behind my house in the shade of a mesquite tree. I didn't even want to bury my dog in Phoenix, but my alternatives were worse. Around his shallow grave were jojoba bushes and small ironwood trees. A paloverde had not burst into bloom, though its time was past, because of the dry winter. All around, doves were moaning back and forth in the brush. Listening to them, the tears of rage and grief sprang into my hot eyes as I sat in the dirt looking at the mound covering Bandit. When I found him dead I had been too busy to feel, but now . . . I thought of Joshua, too, of how much I had liked him before he went crazy, and I thought of Cass Boulding.

After that I spent fifteen minutes loading everything I wanted into the back of my truck before I washed the blood out of it so I would not be detained at Mexican customs. Then I drove south.

Not long after I had turned from my gravel road onto

the pavement, I saw red lights flashing. I stopped behind a yellow school bus.

To the left, a tiny girl in a pink dress hopped down the front steps of a ranch house and ran out a driveway, looked both ways with pride, and ran around the front of the bus. Under one arm she carried a stack of books, and in her other hand she held, very carefully so that nothing would spill out, a wicker basket full of brightly colored eggs.